Penguin Books
The Lie of the Land

Haydn Middleton was born in 1955. He was educated at
Reading School and New College, Oxford, after which
he worked in advertising, publishing and teaching. His
other publications include the novels *The People in the
Picture* (1987) and *The Collapsing Castle* (1990). He lives
in Oxford with his wife and two children.

21/8/95

This interest of yours
is marvellous - really!

Best wishes

Hayd Middleton

The Lie
of the Land

HAYDN MIDDLETON

PENGUIN BOOKS

PENGUIN BOOKS

Published by the Penguin Group
Penguin Books Ltd, 27 Wrights Lane, London W8 5TZ, England
Viking Penguin, a division of Penguin Books USA Inc.,
375 Hudson Street, New York, New York 10014, USA
Penguin Books Australia Ltd, Ringwood, Victoria, Australia
Penguin Books Canada Ltd, 2801 John Street, Markham, Ontario, Canada L3R 1B4
Penguin Books (NZ) Ltd, 182–190 Wairau Road, Auckland 10, New Zealand

Penguin Books Ltd, Registered Offices: Harmondsworth, Middlesex, England

First published by Macmillan London Ltd 1989
Published in Penguin Books 1990
10 9 8 7 6 5 4 3 2 1

Grateful acknowledgement is made to Meibach and Epstein for permission
to reprint lyrics from 'Behind Blue Eyes' by Pete Townshend.
Copyright © 1971 by Eel Pie Publishing Ltd. Reprinted by permission.

Printed in England by Clays Ltd, St Ives plc

For Fiona, with love

For ten years David waited. Then he heard her voice.

I know you, she said. I know you, I have found you, and I will not let you go.

It was all David needed to know. He was going to dance. Already he could see the lips parting, feel the ground shifting, sense the love that was waiting, there, at the end.

And after ten years of waiting he was afraid.

PART ONE

PART ONE

1

On New Year's Day, Quinn served dinner at ten-fifteen. Neither he nor David Nennius ate much. For both men it had been a long evening.

Nennius ran a small electrical installation and repair business. Three hours earlier he had been called out by one of his ladies – the dozen or so elderly widows who turned to him with problems that weren't always electrical. Sometimes a tap needed a new washer, sometimes a heavy piece of furniture had to be moved. Sometimes there wasn't even a problem at all.

Quinn had been defrosting the fridge when he'd heard Nennius start up the van. At once he, too, had left the house, shadowed Nennius across town on his Honda 50, waited in the cold for him to do his work, then followed him back home again. He hated to be so furtive – especially when it turned out that Nennius had only been unblocking a drain. But Quinn had grown reluctant to let the big man out of his sight after dark.

When the meal was over Nennius stayed at the table and smoked cigarettes. Quinn washed the dishes, glancing up at Nennius' reflection in the kitchen window: the slightly hooded blue eyes, the large proud nose, the determined set of his mouth. Although his hair and skin were so fair, he had always reminded Quinn of an eagle – an immense, temporarily grounded bird of prey.

'Would you like coffee, David?' Quinn asked, turning from the sink and drying his hands on a tea-towel.

Nennius shook his head. 'I'm going downstairs.'

'I could bring you a cup.'

Nennius shook his head again and smiled.

Quinn smiled back. Then he began to lay the table for breakfast.

For two weeks Nennius had spent every evening in the basement office – sitting at his desk, staring at the wall, listening to old records, drinking his way through bottle after bottle of whisky. And then, usually long after midnight, he would stagger upstairs and drive off in the van.

Quinn had started to follow him mainly because he feared for his safety. As far as he could tell, Nennius drove just for the sake of driving. Even when he pulled off the road, into lay-bys or outside public conveniences, he stayed inside the van. But whatever he was trying to find – or escape – he didn't appear to be succeeding. Each morning he looked more haunted.

'Breakfast at seven?' Quinn asked as he set Nennius' clean place-mat in front of him.

'Seven will be fine.'

Nennius stubbed out his cigarette and stood. He was six feet eight and a half inches tall, but there was nothing freakish about the look of him. At forty years of age he was in excellent shape: well proportioned, loose-limbed, easy in his movements. He turned to leave the room.

'Good night, then, David,' Quinn said.

Nennius nodded to him from the doorway. Minutes later, a rock song boomed up from the basement. Quinn finished in the kitchen, switched off the lights, and went upstairs to the bathroom.

He showered quickly. Crossing the landing afterwards, he looked into Nennius' bedroom. Although the light wasn't on, the great double bed was bathed in yellow neon from the Chinese takeaway across the street.

The walls were bare except for a single postcard reproduction of a painting, pinned high above the grate. Quinn saw it clearly in the neon glow: a fair-haired man standing naked in front of a sunburst, his arms spread wide in a kind of shrug. *Don't ask me*, the figure seemed to be saying, *I haven't got a clue what's wrong with him, either*.

Quinn looked away and went to his own, much smaller room. Standing by the window, he reached back and pulled off the elastic band that held his hair in a stumpy pony-tail. He couldn't afford to be vain about his appearance – at twenty-four Quinn was a small man, slight and swarthy, a sparrow-hawk to Nennius' eagle – but he liked to think that the pony-tail lent him a certain harmless glamour.

He shook his hair loose and lay down on top of the bed. Nennius' music still surged up the stairs through Quinn's room, through the roof and out into the night. No one ever complained about the noise: the house was adjoined on one side by a small cinema and on the other by a warren of rooms let out to students.

Quinn closed his eyes. He spent hours each day wondering what Nennius' problem might be, but it wasn't in the nature of their relationship to ask so personal a question. In fourteen months together they had always treated each other with an almost ceremonious formality. Quinn knew little about Nennius' present life, still less about his past; Nennius in turn had never enquired about Quinn's sad but unexceptional history before they had met.

Conversation of any kind had not seemed important. Their life in the house had settled of its own accord into a mutually satisfactory routine. Quinn had come to see the two of them as intimate strangers, both essentially loners, but diluting each other's loneliness by living in parallel.

And now, after sharing the house for over a year, they were as far apart and as close together as they had ever been. The only difference was that for two weeks Nennius had been going to pieces.

2

Suddenly the music stopped. Quinn heard Nennius mount the steps from the basement, pause in the hall, then open the back door. At once Quinn went to his window and stood inconspicuously to one side of it.

New snow was settling on the ground. Nennius stood in the centre of the lawn, smoking a cigarette but keeping his hands at his sides. He was wearing his long fawn overcoat and he looked so forlorn: a mighty haunted eagle, lost in dreams of the time when he had flown.

Quinn watched him spit out the cigarette, close his eyes, and pinch the skin at the bridge of his nose. He stood still for almost a minute, with snowflakes falling thickly into his golden hair. Then he walked across to the high cinema wall which ran the length of the garden.

He laid the palms of both hands flat against it, and slowly leaned forward until his brow rested there, too. Quinn gripped the curtain and caught his breath a moment before it happened. He knew that it was going to happen.

Nennius drew back his head. Then he rammed it, hard, into the brickwork.

Quinn watched him career out into the openness of the small garden, towards the rear fence, dragging a handkerchief from his coat pocket. Already there was blood above his eyes. He tilted back his head, holding his handkerchief to his brow to staunch the flow.

Fretfully Quinn stepped back into his room. At that moment the phone rang. He hurried downstairs in his dressing-gown and picked up the receiver in the hall. His legs were trembling

6

so violently that he had to sit down on the mahogany seat.

'Good evening,' said a man whose voice Quinn didn't recognise. 'Might I speak to David?' He had a North Country accent, similar to Nennius'.

'I think he's just gone out,' Quinn told him.

'On the job, is he?' laughed the man, sounding almost relieved. 'Always on the job, our David. Who are you, then?'

'My name's Quinn. Let me just see if David's still here.' He put down the receiver, pulled on his boots in the kitchen, and with some trepidation he opened the back door.

The garden was empty. Quinn walked across the snow-crusted grass to the back gate. He went outside, saw that the van had gone from its parking-place, and looked right and left down the cobbled back-alley. The van was nowhere to be seen. Quinn closed his eyes, pulled the lapels of his dressing-gown together, and went back indoors.

'No,' he said to the man on the phone, 'he's gone. But if you'll give me your name and number I can ask him to call you back.'

'Oh, don't worry about that,' said the man. 'Meredith's the name, but our David won't ring me back. I'm not exactly his favourite person.'

Quinn didn't know what to say. The name Meredith sounded familiar, although he couldn't think why.

'It's been a long time,' Meredith went on. 'A lot of bad blood. I'll try again some time. Happy new year to you now.'

Quinn went back up to his room. Listlessly he undressed and got into bed.

It was only a matter of time before he would go out and look for the van. He turned on to one side, then the other. There was so much he didn't know. So much he didn't *want* to know. Already he felt that by following Nennius he was betraying the trust between them. He just wanted nothing to be different. Change appalled him; and what he and Nennius had so effortlessly built was too precious to be changed in any way.

And he couldn't help wondering whether he himself might be at fault, whether *he* was vexing Nennius by failing to meet some requirement. But he had no clear idea what that requirement might be. He still couldn't be sure why, fourteen months before, Nennius had invited him into his home.

Quinn had come to the town looking for a job. He had hoped to find work on a building site or in a municipal park. But there had been no work of that kind on offer and, being short of cash, he had bedded down in a run-down allotment shed. At dawn on the first day of November he had woken to find an enormous stranger standing over him, his face a picture of confusion.

'Don't hit me!' Quinn had cried, jumping up from his heap of damp matting. 'Please, please, don't hit me!'

But, far from hitting him, Nennius had smiled, shaken his head, and said: 'You don't have to sleep here. I can give you a room. . . .'

The offer seemed unconditional. Quinn had accepted it gratefully, and within days he had started to turn himself into Nennius' housekeeper.

At first he had cooked and cleaned to make up for paying no rent. But soon he found that domestic work suited him. He felt completely at home in Nennius' house, with its dark solid furniture and its beautiful framed pictures. He had found a sense of peace in its rooms that he had never known before – a sense of peace which, until now, he had always presumed that Nennius shared.

He slept fitfully for three-quarters of an hour. Then he heard the drone of a slowing vehicle out in the alley, the crunch of loose chippings under tyres. He saw the momentary glare of headlights on his wall.

He swallowed hard. There was a tightening in his chest. The van door was being slammed. The back door of the house was opening. There were footsteps, first in the hall, then on the creaking stairs up which Nennius' great shadow preceded him, blocking out the light from below. The sound of footsteps ceased. Quinn blinked. He heard Nennius striking a match to light a cigarette. He pictured to himself the wound on the big man's forehead and he longed for it not to be there.

'David,' he called out as Nennius went into the bathroom and turned on the shower. 'Someone rang. A man called Meredith. He said he'd ring again.'

There was no reply. Quinn listened to the water cascading.

'When he rings again,' Nennius called back at last, 'would you mind just putting down the phone?'

Quinn frowned.

Before he could reply, Nennius closed the bathroom door.

3

At nine-thirty on the next evening Nennius swayed up the driveway to the Samaritans Centre. He rang the doorbell twice before he heard someone coming. It was cold out there on the doorstep. Far too cold to be kept waiting. Through the frosted-glass panel he saw a young woman approaching.

'Is Melissa here?' he asked, slurring the words badly, as soon as the door opened.

'Melissa?' the girl replied with a frown. 'Sorry, no.'

Nennius rubbed his hands together. They were encased in a pair of yellow fingerless mittens. Then he thrust them into the pockets of his overcoat. For a moment his head felt quite empty.

'Do you think *I* could be of any help?' asked the girl. Her voice was deep and resonant, like an old-fashioned radio announcer's.

Nennius glanced at her. She had a wide square face, with eyes that looked promisingly alert, and she was offering him help. She opened the door wider, encouraging him to enter. Nennius thought of the alternative: of driving straight back to his office, back to the bottle of whisky and all the loose ends.

'Yes, all right,' he said, stepping inside. 'Thank you.'

The girl closed the door behind him, and led the way across the hall to a free room. She was wearing chunky winter clothes – a large green sweater, a plaid skirt and thick leg-warmers – but inside them she had a conspicuously sinuous line to her body. "You've spoken to Melissa before, have you?' she asked when they were in the room.

Nennius raised his shoulders, closed his eyes and nodded

all at the same time. Seedy with the smell of cigarettes, it was blissfully warm in there after the doorstep.

'I'm Rachel,' said the girl, taking the armchair nearer to the door.

Nennius gazed blearily around the room. Two chairs, a worn pink mat, grey plaster walls brightened by three abstract paintings. With his hands still in his overcoat pockets, he lowered himself into the empty armchair. 'I'm David Victor Nennius,' he said.

'That's a striking name,' Rachel replied, pursing her lips.

Nennius smiled, twisting in the chair until he found a passably comfortable position. 'I'm large, aren't I?' he said as he came to rest. 'Six eight and a half in my stockinged feet.' He smiled again, nervily, this time straight at Rachel. 'People usually want to know, but they don't like to ask.'

Rachel nodded, but didn't smile back. Nennius noticed that her brown eyes were looking at him sympathetically yet entirely without condescension. He was glad that he had come in at last, after his nerve had failed him so many times before. But now that he was inside, not with Melissa but with this girl, he knew he had to make all the running.

Therefore he told her, in the same tone of voice as that in which he had given her his height: 'I'm going to die.'

'Are you ill?' Rachel asked after a pause.

Nennius laughed. A curt throaty laugh which wasn't at all unpleasant. 'I'm not ill,' he assured a patch of the wall high above her head. Then he lowered his gaze until their eyes met.

Rachel leaned back. The skin on her wide face looked impossibly smooth. She wore her tawny hair up, with one or two loose strands hanging down past the line of her jaw. When she realised that Nennius wasn't intending to continue, she said: 'Shall I go and make us both a coffee?'

'Yes, please,' Nennius answered, probing deeper into his overcoat pockets. 'But, while you're out there, don't go looking for me in your files. I wasn't a client of Melissa's, you see. I used to be married to her. I used to be Melissa's husband. Until five minutes ago, I'd never set foot in one of these places in my life.'

Rachel stood, gripped the door-handle and smiled. 'Melissa?' she said. 'Melissa? I don't think I've come across anyone of that name here. Are you sure she's still a Samaritan?'

Nennius shot her a broken smile. 'I know nothing for sure about Melissa now,' he said. 'She just used to come here on Wednesday evenings, to do her shift, and I looked after the boy. Sometimes she stayed overnight.' He looked down. 'But this was all a long time ago.'

'Coffee,' Rachel said decisively, looking him up and down. 'Milk and sugar?' He nodded to both.

When she came back with the two steaming mugs Nennius had nearly dozed off. He gulped his coffee, spilling some on to his chin, and on to the tracksuit which he wore beneath his overcoat. Absently he rubbed at the dark blue material with his fingertips. Then he drew a packet of cigarettes from his coat pocket. He proffered it to Rachel, who shook her head but handed him an ashtray from the floor.

'David,' she said as he lit up, 'you said to me, before, that you were going to die. Can I ask you why you said that? You . . . you told me you weren't ill.'

Nennius exhaled a long jet of smoke. 'Not ill,' he said, 'no.' He looked as if he were about to roar with laughter. But when he saw how evenly Rachel was regarding him he composed his face at once.

Rachel broke the lengthy silence which followed. 'Did you', she asked, 'come here tonight to tell Melissa why you were going to die?'

Nennius smiled, a little sheepishly. He raised a hand to the plaster on his forehead, then let it fall. 'If Melissa had been here,' he replied, 'I was going to tell her about someone. Someone who has recently been in contact with me.'

'Could you talk to *me* about this person? I mean, is it a man or a woman?'

Nennius gave her an appraising look. She had curled her legs beneath her in the chair and was holding her mug, in both hands, close to her face. Nennius noticed her wedding ring. He liked this girl. She was probably not much older than Quinn, but there was a pleasing maturity, a wholly proper seriousness, to her. In a burst of energy he finished his

12

coffee, set down the mug, swept up hugely out of the chair and headed for the window, where he plucked at one of the curtains.

Outside, the slush was freezing on the pavements. There was very little traffic. He let go of the curtain and turned. 'Believe me,' he said stubbing out his cigarette in the ashtray which he had carried from his chair, 'it isn't easy to talk about this.'

Rachel nodded curtly, as if to show that she had taken as much for granted from the start. 'You said that someone has been in contact,' she persisted. 'And you talk of dying. David, are you thinking of taking your own life? Is it something to do with this person?'

Nennius peered into the ashtray, considering her questions. 'The person . . .,' he began, wincing. 'The *woman*. . . . She's more like the keeper of the gateway to hell.'

'Right,' Rachel said slowly. 'But could I ask you again – are you thinking of taking your own life?'

Nennius looked at her with a wry gaunt smile. Then he shook his head.

'Then, who, exactly,' Rachel asked, 'is going to kill you?'

'Not who,' Nennius told her. 'It's not exactly *who*.'

'Go on.'

Rachel's expression tightened. Nennius' eyes were fixed on hers, although his smile passed right through her. Suddenly he rubbed his forehead and raised his eyebrows.

'I know I've got to die, Rachel,' he said, 'but I'm a coward.' He shrugged dismissively. 'I'm afraid.' He shrugged again. 'And I really have to be going now.'

Shaking his head, he walked across the room. As he opened the door, Rachel rose from her chair. '*Why* have you got to die?' she asked his massive back.

He half-turned towards her. 'Because of what I've done,' he said. 'Because of who I am.'

Rachel's expression did not falter. 'What is it that you've done, David?'

He looked at her for several moments, and then he looked away, quickly, as if he had seen something in her face which had taken him unawares. 'Thanks for listening to me,' he said, pulling the door back, 'and for the coffee.'

As he moved out into the hall ahead of her the front door was being unlocked from the outside. A thin man with lank grey hair came in, swearing at the cold. He carried a rolled-up sleeping-bag.

'Here comes the night-shift!' said Nennius.

The thin man chuckled back, passed on and climbed the stairs two at a time.

Back on the doorstep Nennius ran a hand through his tousled fair hair. The coffee had started to sober him up. 'I may be back,' he told Rachel with a grin, 'now that I'm on the files.'

'I'd be pleased to talk with you again,' she replied. 'So would any of the others here, whenever you feel like it. And you can always phone.'

'Yes. I can always do that.' Nennius buttoned his overcoat and turned up the collar. Rachel watched, leaning against the door-frame, her arms folded tightly across her chest.

They smiled, wished each other a happy new year, and Nennius walked down the driveway. He turned the corner into the cul-de-sac where his van was waiting. *D. V. Nennius*, said the flaked Gothic lettering on the left-hand side-panel. *AYE – All Your Electrics*, it said on the right. And he had left the lights on.

He climbed in and pressed his face into his hands. It had done no good. The words and the love were too far beyond him. He hadn't even come close.

He edged the van forward, turned out of the cul-de-sac, and drove away.

It was only when Nennius had driven right around the curve of the road that a very cold Quinn emerged from behind a tree in the smaller road opposite the Centre.

He jogged fifty yards to the place where he'd left his Honda after tailing Nennius from the house. He had seen enough. And what he had seen had puzzled him, but it had also given him grounds for hope.

4

As soon as Nennius turned out of the driveway, Rachel closed the front door of the Samaritans Centre.

She went back into the room where they had spoken, collected the coffee-mugs and took them up to the kitchen. Climbing the stairs, she shut her eyes as a motorbike accelerated noisily past the front of the building. She washed the cups and went through to the room where the files were kept.

The lank-haired man, seated at one of two tables, was taking a phone call, without having had time to remove his anorak. He raised his hand in silent greeting, then watched as Rachel took two blank cards from the bank of filing-cabinets. A large middle-aged woman was sitting at the second table, deep in a different telephone conversation. She didn't look up.

Rachel perched on the edge of the single bed, and began to make out the first card on her lap. She headed it with a reference number, entered the date, paused for a moment, then continued. She wrote quickly but with a certain relish. Filling in these cards made a welcome change from the more formal documents that, as a solicitor, she composed to make her living.

Extremely tall, Rachel wrote beneath the reference number. *Fair-haired, pale-skinned. In his late 30s, possibly early 40s, softly spoken with a faint northern accent. Although he's so big, he seemed to me very gentle. He was drunk tonight. There was a plaster across his forehead.*

He believes that he's going to die, and came here looking for his ex(?) wife, a Melissa, who used to be a Sam. He wanted to tell her about some other woman. He seems to think this woman is going to be involved in killing him. I had the impression that he was quite anxious to say more.

Rachel then took the second card, headed it *David Victor Nennius*, repeated her physical description, and gave a cross-reference to her other card. By the time she had finished writing, she was already ten minutes over the end of her shift. After filing the cards she went through to the next room, where she had to ring the leader and report back on the evening's events.

She sat down and dialled his number. The leader that night was an avuncular man in his mid-thirties called Alasdair. Rachel knew him well. Her husband had once been a colleague of his in an academic publishing firm.

'Anyone difficult tonight?' Alasdair asked.

'No, not really,' said Rachel. 'And just one new client. A guy of forty or so. David Nennius. I have a feeling he'll be back. He stayed for about twenty minutes, but only opened up towards the end. I think he took himself by surprise actually, and decided to make a quick getaway before he said too much But he seemed to want to talk in spite of himself.'

'What was on his mind?'

'He thinks he's going to die. But he says he's not ill.'

'Suicide, then?'

'It's a possibility. He seemed to have woman trouble. As a matter of fact, he came here asking for his ex-wife, someone called Melissa. He said she used to be a Sam, years ago. It could have been pure fabrication of course, something to help him to get as far as the door. He seemed to lose interest in her once he was inside.'

'Melissa? It doesn't ring any bells. But I'll ask around. What did you say the fellow's surname was?'

'Nennius.'

'I thought you did. It's unusual.' He paused. 'Wasn't there a Dark Age historian called Nennius? A monk?'

Rachel shrugged. 'Quite possibly. Maggie would be the one to ask.' Maggie, Alasdair's wife, was the editor of a small history journal.

'Yes, indeed. So tell me – what kind of a chap is this David?'

'Well, he's absolutely enormous. Six feet eight and a half, he told me.'

'Good God!'

'And he was well dressed – at least, his clothes looked expensive. Not at all badly spoken, very polite. But he'd been drinking, quite heavily by the sound and smell of him, so I couldn't really tell how seriously he meant what he was saying.'

'Right. So basically he said he had woman problems and that he was expecting to die?'

'There were some other things, too. But, as I say, I'm not sure whether that was just the drink talking.'

'What things were these, Rachel? Oh, look, I'm terribly sorry, are you in a hurry to get off now?'

'No, no,' lied Rachel. Her husband, Matthew, hated her to be out on her bicycle after dark. He fretted if she were even a couple of minutes late home. But Rachel saw no point in doing this work unless she were to do it thoroughly.

'How serious a suicide possibility do you think this is?' said Alasdair. 'Did he give you anything else to go on?'

'Well, he did say that a woman had recently been in contact with him, and that she was "like the keeper of the gateway to hell".'

'Did he now?'

'And he seemed to feel guilty about something. He wouldn't be drawn, but he appears to believe that he *deserves* to die.'

'I see,' said Alasdair. 'Well, if you think he's likely to come back, maybe we'll be able to find out a bit more. I'll ask around to see if there ever was a Melissa. You never know. . . .' He sighed. 'Anyway, Rachel, how's Matthew? Do you know – I don't think I've seen him since your wedding. I heard that he'd gone into market research. Is that right?'

Rachel closed her eyes and smiled. Just over a year earlier – and two weeks before she married him – Matthew had been made redundant by his firm. 'Yes,' she said, 'he is doing some work for an agency. It's not what he wants to be doing, of course, figure-bashing. In fact he's awfully scathing about it. But the money's reasonable. And he thinks it'll tide him over until he can get back into publishing.'

'He was unlucky,' said Alasdair. 'It can't have been easy – adjusting.'

'No,' said Rachel, attempting to sound noncommittal. She wasn't the person to admit that the redundancy had blighted their entire brief marriage. 'Look,' she went on, 'you should come round some time with Maggie. We'd love to see you. I'll fix a date with Matthew and give you a ring, shall I? Come to dinner.' She stood. 'Actually, I should be getting back to him now. He panics if I don't get home on the dot. He thinks no one's safe on the streets after about eight o'clock!'

'There could be something in that. But it would be splendid to get together again. Sorry I've held you up now. And a happy new year to you both.'

Quickly Rachel went back into the other room to fetch her duffel coat. The lank-haired man was still talking to his first caller. He smiled and waved goodbye to Rachel. The large woman beamed and bade her good night, too.

Rachel pulled on her coat as she hurried down the stairs. She was leaving the Centre more than twenty minutes later than she usually did. And she knew exactly how Matthew would be when she returned: quiet, aggrieved, waiting to suggest, yet again, that she should consider taking on some good work which was less potentially hazardous.

She raised her hood, buttoned her coat up to her chin, then went out into the bitter night to unlock her bicycle.

5

Rachel's in-laws came to stay for the first weekend of the new year. They were a pleasant couple, the proprietors of a fish and chip restaurant on the south coast. Rachel liked them, but they were intimidated by the fact that she was a professional person with a university degree. Sadder still, they always seemed overawed by their own son's intelligence.

They had never before stayed overnight in Matthew's flat. Rachel still thought of it as Matthew's flat, despite having lived in it for eighteen months, as his lover and then as his wife. It comprised the ground floor of a semi-detached house in the town's fashionable northern suburb.

By Saturday evening the four of them were running out of things to talk about. On Sunday morning, the atmosphere became uneasy. While Rachel and her in-laws took down the Christmas decorations and prepared lunch, Matthew typed in his study. Even though he left the door open, he isolated himself from the others by erecting his customary wall of music. Ever since losing his job he had found it hard to face his parents. Rachel assured him repeatedly that they were in no way disappointed in him. But she knew it went deeper than that: he was disappointed in himself on their behalf, and Rachel could say nothing to change that.

Over lunch Matthew's mother asked him what he had been working on that morning. He shrugged dismissively. When Rachel then probed him gently, he became embarrassed and changed the subject.

Rachel suspected that he was writing a novel. He had often spoken of his intention to do so. He had even outlined a plot to her: a kind of fantasy, with what sounded like an autobiographical premiss. She had mixed feelings about Matthew as a would-be novelist. He had lots of interesting ideas, but was a physicist by training and an editor of scientific monographs by experience. It was feasible that he had a good novel in him. It was equally feasible, however, that his work wouldn't find favour with a publisher. And Rachel shrank from thinking how his corroded ego might react to rejection in the wake of redundancy.

After lunch, while she was grinding beans for coffee, the phone rang.

Matthew went through to his study and took the call. Moments later he returned to the kitchen-diner. 'It's for you,' he said to Rachel, wrinkling his forehead. 'Grace?'

Rachel frowned back. She could think of no Grace who would ring her at home on Sunday.

In the study Davis, Matthew's ageing sheltie dog, was asleep in his basket. 'Hello?' Rachel said, sitting at the untidy desk. Out of habit she picked up a pencil and scanned the clutter for a slip of paper to write on, taking care not to read anything which Matthew mightn't have wanted her to read.

'It's Grace,' said a woman with a small quavering voice. 'We have met, but I don't expect you'll remember me. At the Centre. I'm not a Sam any more now, but we were on duty together once or twice.'

'Oh, I do remember you,' Rachel told her. 'Yes, I do.' She was recalling a sick-looking old woman with bluish hair, bulbous eyes, and glasses on a chain around her neck.

'I'm awfully sorry to be bothering you like this,' said the woman. 'Tell me if it's inconvenient and I'll ring off at once.'

'No, please. What's the problem?'

'Well, it's not a problem really. It's just that Alasdair spoke to my husband yesterday. My husband's still a Sam, you see, and I got to hear that you'd had a client come in who was asking for Melissa. . . .'

'Ah, yes! So do you know? Was there ever such a person?'

The woman paused before answering. 'Oh, yes. She was a West Indian girl. Very elegant, very pretty.'

Rachel nodded. 'That's interesting,' she said, doodling on

the back of an envelope. 'I'll admit I wasn't inclined to believe the client at the time.'

'Oh, no, there definitely was a Melissa, and she definitely was married to that great big man. I saw him once, at a Sams barbecue. David. There was a son, too. He had a peculiar name. I suppose he must have been five or six when I saw him. But this was, oh, ten years ago now. Ten at least.'

'This does put a new complexion on things,' Rachel said, doodling more quickly. 'The more I've thought about the client, the more I've worried that he wouldn't talk to me. There's a chance that he's contemplating suicide, you see. I don't suppose you'd know where we could find Melissa now? Would it be possible to contact her, to let her know he's looking for her?'

Grace hesitated, then she said: 'That would be difficult. She went up north somewhere after the marriage broke up – to a relative, I think – and she took the child with her. I've got no address, I'm afraid.' She paused. 'I suppose it's *possible* that she might have come back.' Again she paused, momentarily, as if she were gauging how much she could allow herself to divulge. 'I doubt that, though, somehow.'

'Oh,' said Rachel, interested, 'why is that? I'm sorry, hold on a moment.'

She placed her hand over the mouthpiece, and smiled up at Matthew, who had brought in her glass of wine. He set it down carefully beside the envelope on which she was making her scribbles.

'Thanks,' Rachel whispered to him. 'It's Sams. I won't be a moment.'

Matthew kissed the crown of her head. 'There's no hurry,' he said. As he turned to leave, Rachel took his hand and squeezed it. He grinned down at her, nodded and raised his eyebrows, then went back in to his parents.

'Sorry,' Rachel said to Grace. 'But I was wondering why you felt that Melissa wouldn't have come back. Do you actually know what happened between her and the client?'

There was then such a silence at the end of the line that Rachel felt bound to say: 'Hello? Are you still there?'

'Yes, I'm here,' said Grace, her voice faltering even more noticeably than before. 'This is rather difficult for me. I'm sorry.' She paused yet again, lengthily. 'I didn't know Melissa particularly well or anything. I'd seen her at the Centre a few times, and at this barbecue thing. That was all. But when her marriage was breaking up, you see, she came to talk to me. At the Centre, as a client. She was dreadfully disturbed. And what she told me then was told in confidence.'

Rachel sipped some wine, and tried to sound persuasive rather than peevish when she answered. 'Yes, I do appreciate that. But it's no breach of confidence to discuss with another Samaritan what she said to you, is it?'

'I'm afraid I'm not explaining things properly,' Grace replied. 'Melissa was adamant that our conversation should go no further. In fact she refused to say a word unless I agreed to that in advance. I know I should never have gone along with it. It's most irregular. But because she was in such a frightful state I did.' She cleared her throat. 'It hasn't been easy to keep my word.'

Davis shifted himself in his basket. Rachel sipped some more wine. She put down her glass and picked up the pencil. At this stage it wasn't clear to her why Grace had chosen to phone. If it was just a question of confirming that Melissa existed, she could have passed on a note via her husband. Something else had to be bothering her, and Rachel was interested to know what it was.

'Is there anything, Grace, that you feel you *can* say to me? Anything that might conceivably be of help to the client?'

'It's not on account of the client that I'm ringing you,' Grace replied with surprising tartness.

'I'm not quite sure I follow.'

'Oh dear, this is so messy. I really am most terribly torn.' She cleared her throat again. 'All I wanted to tell you was to be very careful, Rachel. The client, this David, he's a dangerous man. You'll just have to take that on trust. But please believe me, I'm telling you the truth.'

'Dangerous?' Rachel repeated dully.

'He's capable of doing the most awful damage, Rachel.'

Neither woman spoke for some moments.

'There really isn't anything else I can tell you,' Grace said in the end. 'I know it's unsatisfactory, but I felt I had to talk to you. I've said nothing about any of this to Alasdair or even to my husband, and I'd prefer it if you didn't, either. Already I've let Melissa down by saying as much as I have. But you will take care, won't you, if he should come back?'

'Yes,' said Rachel. 'Yes, I will. And thank you.'

Rachel didn't go straight back into the kitchen-diner. Instead she sat doodling on the envelope until it was almost entirely smothered with arrow-headed coils. Grace's warning hadn't bothered her unduly. She remembered now the perpetually harassed look on the little old woman's face; and she really was quite old, probably in her late seventies. It was arguable that she'd remembered some fragments of her conversation with Melissa, then reconstructed them into something altogether more distressing.

Rachel fingered the rim of her wine-glass. She knew full well that she was giving her client the benefit of the doubt. There was no denying that David Nennius had left a strong impression – both visual and verbal – on her. And, as she had mentioned to Grace, since Wednesday she had grown increasingly concerned about him.

In her own mind there was now little doubt that he was a potential suicide. He had definitely looked to her like a victim, even though this didn't square with what Grace had attempted to tell her. She knew that she would have to keep the old lady's cryptic tip-off in mind. But, far from fretting about seeing Nennius again, she was now keener than before for him to come back. She wanted the chance to chat with him again, to make a better shot at encouraging him to say whatever it was that he needed to say.

6

At nine o'clock on Sunday evening Nennius finished taking down the Christmas lights in a small shopping precinct.

It was dishearteningly cold. With numb hands he dismantled the high ladder and fixed it to the top of the van. As he climbed up into the cabin, Quinn came back from the burger bar with their supper. They ate the food quickly, listening to the weather reports on the radio. Rain was on the way, then more snow. Nennius eased the van out on to the icy main road.

'There's one more job I ought to do,' he said to Quinn. He reached down for his packet of cigarettes, shook it, and found that it was empty. 'It'll only take a few minutes. Fitting a new door-bell. Do you mind?'

'I don't mind, David,' said Quinn. 'That's fine.'

Quinn wasn't sure why Nennius had asked him along that night. There had been virtually nothing for him to do in the shopping precinct, and Nennius was quite capable of fitting a door-bell on his own. The big man seemed very edgy. Quinn noticed that he was gripping the steering-wheel so hard that his knuckles were white.

They drew up in a wide road in which the tall terraced houses were set some way back from the pavement. Nennius took his tools from the bag on the floor of the cab. 'This won't take long,' he said.

'Shall I stay here, then?' asked Quinn.

'No, I'd like you to come in. Is that all right?'

Quinn, hearing an unevenness in the older man's voice, opened his door at once. The road was ankle-deep in slush. It had begun to rain again. The girl who answered the door kissed

Nennius on the cheek. Then she noticed Quinn, smiled, and said hello. Quinn saw the disappointment in her smile. They went straight through to the kitchen. The girl sat at the table while Nennius produced a small box from his coat pocket.

'I've brought you a new bell,' he said, setting it down in front of her and nodding at the gong-and-hammer fixture above the kitchen door. 'That old thing can't cope with the current.'

The girl gazed accusingly into his eyes. Nennius blushed, grinned, then set about his work. Until the time came to test the new bell, Quinn was embarrassingly superfluous. For ten minutes the three of them kept up an almost complete silence. Now and then Quinn caught the girl's eye, and she would smile at him. But mostly she watched Nennius.

Quinn had met this girl several times before. She was in her late twenties, petite and attractive, and although she wore a wedding ring Quinn knew that she now lived alone. Quinn liked her well enough. He also understood that she wanted more from Nennius than Nennius was prepared to give her. Two or three times, late at night, she had come to the house uninvited. Quinn had always turned her away, explaining (as Nennius had asked him to explain) that David was out on call.

Quinn hadn't worried about lying; he saw the lies as part of a larger truth – that Nennius, despite having once been married, was ill at ease with younger women, especially attractive young women who liked him. Quinn sympathised: he had never been comfortable with girls himself, although in his case the wariness had usually been mutual.

Within a quarter of an hour, Nennius had the new bell working.

'I won't charge you for the call-out,' he said, glancing down the hall at the front door. 'Just for the cost of the bell.'

The girl stood. She took one step in his direction, passing Quinn. 'I thought we might go for a drink, David,' she said. 'We haven't had a drink for ages.' Quinn could tell how much it was costing her to say this in front of him.

But Nennius had already moved out into the hall, abstractedly putting his tools into his coat pocket, then taking them out again. The set of his face was wild. Quinn had never seen that look on him before. It seemed entirely inappropriate. 'I'm sorry,' Nennius said, looking away. 'We have to be going.'

He was in the front garden before Quinn could squeeze past the girl, who had remained in the kitchen doorway.

'Goodbye,' he said to her, turning, with his hand on the front door. He wanted to apologise on Nennius' behalf, tell her that Nennius had no grievance against *her*, explain that the big man was going through some kind of crisis. The girl smiled at him, raised one hand, and fluttered her fingers. And Quinn could only smile back. Then he closed the door.

The rain was falling harder. Quinn ran through the slush to the van. Nennius, bent forward as if he were nursing a wound in his stomach, had opened the passenger-door.

'Please,' he called to Quinn, throwing him the keys. 'Would you drive?'

When Quinn started the engine, Nennius tried to curl himself up inside his coat. His lips were parted, his eyes closed tight. He seemed to be having trouble with his breathing.

Quinn pulled out, alarmed. 'Straight home?' he asked.

Nennius shook his head, took several deep breaths, then directed Quinn to the main southbound carriageway out of town. After Quinn had driven a short way along it, Nennius indicated that he should pull into a lay-by.

Nennius unfastened his seat-belt while Quinn looked through the rain at the prefabricated lavatory building at the end of the lay-by. The single word *Knives* had been aerosoled massively on to its front wall. The surrounding snow-carpet was pockmarked with footprints. Discarded sherry- and cider-bottles nestled in their own deeper recesses.

'Would you wait here?' Nennius said, wincing.

Then he slid out of the cabin, and walked, still knotted up, towards the men's entrance. A faint light showed behind the strip of opaque glass just below the building's roof. Back out on the road, in and around the bus shelter, half a dozen intrepid alcoholics were holding their regular party.

Quinn turned off the engine but left on the lights. He drummed his fingers on the steering-wheel. He couldn't understand why Nennius hadn't used the bathroom in the girl's house, or even waited fifteen minutes until they'd got home. He eyed the cavorting drunks. They made him feel nervous. The whole place made him uneasy. He would greatly have preferred it if Nennius had asked to be taken back to the Samaritans Centre.

Quinn was glad that Nennius had gone in search of constructive help on Wednesday evening. He didn't know much about the Samaritans or the way they operated, but they were surely the right kind of people for Nennius to have gone to. It surprised Quinn, however, that he had turned to a girl in his time of need. And even from behind his tree it had been clear that she was very pretty, too. He hadn't been able to stop thinking about that.

He switched on the van's radio. The rock music oppressed him and, because he didn't want to change Nennius' station setting, he switched it off again. When Nennius had been inside for five minutes, one of the alcoholics peeled away from the bus-shelter group and headed for the lavatory.

He crossed right in front of the van's lights. Quinn saw that he was young – probably under thirty, with long hair and a longer, matted beard – and he was carrying a large bottle by its neck.

On an impulse Quinn climbed down from the cab, slammed the door, and followed the man towards the entrance. He kept his eyes on the huge letters of the word *Knives*. The man disappeared inside. *I just wanted to check that you were all right*, Quinn rehearsed under his breath as he made to follow. *I just came to see if you were all right. . . .*

He heard the first muffled shout before he was out of the rain. Running forward, he heard glass shattering.

'David!' he cried.

The light was dazzlingly bright inside. The sodden tiled floor was littered with the glass of the broken bottle. Nennius had his great back to Quinn. With one hand he had pinned the moaning drunk to the far wall. With the fist of the other he was jabbing at his face, neck and chest.

'David!' Quinn said again, incredulous. But Nennius didn't hear. As the bearded man slumped down the wall, silent now, Nennius was bending his knees, punching lower. At last he allowed him to collapse on to the floor.

'Oh, David!' Quinn breathed.

Nennius turned, pushing back his hair. His mouth was open, his nostrils flaring, his eyes hard and bright. He seemed to be laughing, although Quinn, taking one step back, knew that this had nothing to do with fun.

The bearded alcoholic had revived himself. He was rolling his head, whimpering, pleading. Quinn watched the motion of his broken lips. 'You've got the wrong man,' he said through the blood.

Nennius stooped and heaved him up by his hair and the collar of his jacket. Then he dashed his head against the side of the nearest urinal.

'That's *enough*, David!' Quinn begged him, stepping back again, not daring to remain so close. 'Let's go now. Please let's go.'

Nennius let the sobbing man fall again to the floor. Then he turned on Quinn. 'Don't speak,' he instructed him. He rolled his shoulders to make his coat sit properly, cleared his throat, and strode out into the rain.

Quinn ran after him. Three of the other alcoholics were already straggling towards the lavatory building. Quinn rushed around to the driver's side of the van. He started the engine before Nennius had belted himself in.

'What did he *do* to you, David?' he asked dazedly when they were back on the road.

Nennius was flushed, throbbing, playing with his fingers, but he seemed to be regaining possession of himself. 'He did nothing,' he replied, reaching for his cigarette-packet then remembering that it was empty.

Quinn hesitated before speaking again. 'But what on earth was happening in there?'

Nennius turned to Quinn, and their eyes met. 'Let's just get home,' he said. 'We'll talk at home.'

Quinn looked away, at the road and at the rain. Nennius switched on the radio. Neither of them said another word until they were inside the house.

'I need a shower,' Nennius said in the hall. Still in his coat, he climbed the stairs quickly. Quinn followed. On the landing he turned into his bedroom.

Trembling, he lay on top of his bed in the dark while Nennius cleaned himself up. Gradually, listening to the gushing of the water, a stillness returned to Quinn's body. He made himself think of nothing. He could afford to think of nothing. Nothing but the water, and the light out on the landing, and the expectation of an explanation. Nothing but that.

Nennius was a long time in the shower. He dressed in his bedroom before at last he came to Quinn's room, knocked, and came in rubbing at his hair with a towel. He perched on the end of the bed. And then, to the younger man's astonishment, he closed his hand gently around Quinn's stockinged foot. Quinn tensed himself, but Nennius retained his grip. They sat in silence for several minutes. Nennius dropped the towel and ran his free hand over the plaster on his forehead. Quinn propped himself up on his elbows, watching, waiting.

'I would like', Nennius said in a soft controlled voice, 'to tell you a story. An old story. About a child from an eastern land, called Brutus.'

Quinn's face darkened, but Nennius bowed his head and went on: 'When he was still in his mother's womb, it was prophesied that he would be the child of death, that he would kill his father and mother, and be hateful to all men. . . .'

'David!' Quinn said in disbelief, withdrawing his foot from Nennius' grasp. The word came out hoarsely. Suddenly he felt very cold. He sat up and tucked both knees under his chin. He tried to smile, but Nennius simply gazed back into his face, then stood.

Quinn pressed his forehead into his knees and closed his eyes. Oh Christ, don't be mad, David, he prayed. Please, please, don't be mad.

'In due course,' Nennius continued, stepping across to the window and bending to stare out into the night, 'Brutus' mother died in giving birth to him. Some time later, he killed his father in a hunting accident. So the people drove him out of the land, and for years he sailed the seas, gathering other exiles around him, fighting in wars, marrying a woman against her will. . . .' He peered curiously through the window at a car crawling along the back alley.

Stop it! Quinn wanted to moan into his knees. Stop it, stop it, stop it! But he was too stupefied to say a word. He just gripped his own ankles, and saw again the bearded alcoholic's head, bouncing back off the side of the urinal. A cold-blooded act of violence committed by a completely sober man. And now that same man was telling him a bedtime story. *Don't be mad, David!*

'The child of death came at last to a temple. There he heard a voice, a woman's voice, sweet and inviting. The voice told of an island beyond the setting of the sun. A perfect empty island that was waiting for him and for all those who would ever be like him, guilty and innocent alike. An island of rocky shores, where all things had begun and all things would end. . . .'

Quinn opened his eyes. A film of tears had formed over them. He glared at his feet and the duvet beneath them. He had stopped listening. The story meant nothing to him. But he was intending to let Nennius finish. Then he would speak. He would have to speak. This was now too serious for silence.

'Brutus and his exiles sailed west until at last they reached their promised island. They stepped ashore.' Nennius paused. 'Brutus took the island for himself, and he named it Britain, after himself. But there was an island inside the island, and this darker inner island was Albion. It always had been and always would be. And the island of Albion consumed Brutus the Hateful. It closed over each of those who came with him, and all those who ever came west after him. All the millions, all through the centuries. Here, here. Always here.'

He turned his eyes on Quinn. 'This is the island of the child of death, Quinn,' he said. 'This is the end of the earth, these are the uplands of hell. I know that.'

Quinn raised his head, blinking furiously. 'Could you now tell me, David,' he said, paying out each word as if his question were a length of rope, 'what happened in that lavatory this evening?'

Nennius picked up his towel and crossed to the doorway. 'I've told you as much as I can,' he said.

'But you've only told me a story!'

Nennius smiled. 'I'm sorry, Quinn,' he said, and his smile dissolved into an expression of genuine distress. 'I've told you everything that matters.'

7

For the next three days Nennius rarely left the office. He
disconnected his phone. He wanted no meals. He didn't sleep.
For long periods Quinn watched him from the darkness of the
adjoining workshop. All he seemed to need was his music and
his whisky.

From time to time he worked at the word processor
on which he typed his business letters. More often he sat
motionless but alert in his chair. It was as if he were waiting
in there for something to happen, and Quinn couldn't find the
courage to disturb him. So no more was said about the fight.
No more was said about the impenetrable story. Intermittently
Quinn convinced himself that the entire evening had been a
delusion.

But it *had* happened. All of it. And Quinn spent a great part
of those three days agonising over what he could do next. He
admitted that he had been swept some way out of his depth.
On his own he felt helpless. He needed to talk to someone –
someone who might know more about Nennius than he did.
At eight on Wednesday evening, he left the house and rode
fast into the south side of town.

He had high hopes that the girl would be on duty. After
all, it had been on the previous Wednesday that Nennius had
gone inside and talked with her. It was important that the girl
should be there. In the light of Sunday's developments, it had
become very important.

He parked his bike behind the same tree as before, then
watched the Centre. It was a big detached house on a corner,
three-storeyed, set in a shrub-filled garden. Soon the front

door opened. A woman came out. She was slim and had a baby in a sling around her neck. She stood for several minutes on the doorstep, talking to someone whom Quinn couldn't quite see. Then she came away, and the person inside stepped into view before waving goodbye. It was the pretty girl.

She was dressed in jeans and a blouse this time and she had her hair down, but Quinn recognised her. He crossed the road, passed the woman with the baby, went to the door and rang the bell. The girl came.

'Hello,' she said with a smile, glancing from his face to the crash-helmet in his hand.

'Hello,' said Quinn. 'I'd like to talk to you, if that would be all right?'

The girl pulled back the door, and Quinn went in. He followed her into a large room and sat in the chair which she offered him.

'My name is Rachel,' she said, sitting. Quinn allowed himself to look into her face. She was really quite beautiful. A week before he had been full of admiration for her poise in the doorway. In an odd way she had reminded him of that serene fair-haired man on the postcard in Nennius' bedroom. But, close to, her face was far more lovely, far more open and inviting than the fair-haired man's. And her skin looked quite fabulously smooth.

'I'm Quinn,' he said, looking away.

'Is that your first or second name?'

Quinn shrugged. 'It's my second name. I've got a first name but I prefer to be called Quinn.'

She shrugged back. 'That's fine.'

A longish silence followed.

'Look,' said Quinn, clamping both hands on to the crash-helmet in his lap, 'I've come here because I think we might be able to help each other.'

Rachel raised her eyebrows, then smiled cordially, but said nothing.

Quinn had presumed that the Samaritans started off these sessions by asking questions, or at least by saying *something*. He glared at the abstract painting on the wall ahead of him.

Then he looked down at his gloved hands and began to rock gently back and forth.

'I don't want to give you the wrong impression,' he said. 'I haven't got a problem myself. I'm here because of David, because I'm worried about him.'

'David?' asked Rachel, crossing her legs and leaning forward a little.

'David Nennius, the electrician. You know – he came to see you last week?'

Rachel clasped her hands over her higher knee, and for several moments she stared at the carpet. Quinn, still rocking, became too tense to wait for an answer. It would serve no one's purpose if she denied that Nennius had come to her.

'It's OK,' he said quickly, in an attempt to move things along, 'I know he was here because I saw him. I live with him, you see, in his house. And last Wednesday evening he went out around nine. Well, I followed him on my bike – because he's been so . . . so strange recently – and he came here. I saw you let him in and I saw him coming out again afterwards.' He smiled.

Rachel uncrossed her legs and looked at Quinn with patient incredulity.

'Quinn,' she said quietly, 'I honestly can't say anything about what you saw or didn't see last week. If somebody comes here, then everything about their visit has to be treated in the strictest confidence. That's the way things are, I'm afraid.'

They looked at each other. Quinn felt horribly crushed.

'Could you,' Rachel then began again, 'could you possibly tell me a bit about yourself, do you think?'

Quinn stopped rocking and drummed his fingers on the crash-helmet. A bus passed the building, making something concealed in the room vibrate noisily. He watched Rachel sit back in her chair, smiling, still eyeing him. A lump was forming in his throat. 'He told you what was the matter with him, did he?' he said in a cracked voice, glaring at the painting.

Rachel smiled and, rather too quickly, raised a hand to her cheek. 'Please, Quinn,' she said. 'There's just no way I can talk to you about this. . . .'

'Because, you see,' Quinn interrupted her, the pitch of his

voice rising ominously, 'he won't tell me what's going on. All he's told me is a mad story. And I'm getting frightened, you see. That's why I watch him, you see, and follow him, and . . . and then the other night he was in a fight. . . .'

He halted abruptly. He could feel the lump in his throat swelling, and he didn't want this girl to write him off as a hysteric. He simply wanted her to pool her resources with his. It seemed such a little thing to ask, playing as they were for stakes which were so very high.

Rachel sat forward. 'Would you like a cup of coffee?' she asked.

'No,' Quinn virtually shouted back at her, then he recovered himself sufficiently to add, 'thank you.' He looked into her face. 'All I want is for David to be all right again. That's the only reason I came here. And if you won't talk to me about him, then I might as well go.'

Rachel screwed up her face. For a moment Quinn believed that she was going to relent. She nodded slowly at him. 'I know this isn't what you want to hear, Quinn,' she went on, 'but could you give me a slightly clearer idea of what it is that you're . . . frightened about?'

Quinn stood, swarming with frustration, and he took a step towards Rachel. 'I've *told* you what I'm frightened about. I'm frightened because I don't know what's wrong with David. And I want him to be all right. I'd have thought that you would have wanted that, too.'

Rachel looked up impassively from her chair. Their eyes met. Quinn wished he could have seen inside her head, just to find out how much she knew. But he didn't dislike this girl. Beautiful and confident though she was, he didn't feel at all threatened by her. And he appreciated that she was only doing what she thought was the right thing. In this case, however, the right thing just wasn't good enough. He turned and made for the door.

Rachel followed him wordlessly out of the room and watched as he let himself out of the building. He didn't look back as he walked then trotted down the driveway. He was close to tears. On the ride back through town, beneath the din of his machine, he kept his hold only by spitting and swearing and moaning into the face of the unconcerned night.

He wheeled his bike into the garden shed, careful not to scrape the only other vehicle inside – a woman's bicycle that Nennius had recently been overhauling, ready to sell.

Quinn couldn't feel angry with the girl at the Centre. *Things* could make him angry, but very rarely people. He was disappointed at having failed with Rachel but he hadn't given up on her. Under the protocol she had been, he sensed, sympathetic. Already he was imagining that he might go back to her. He owed it to all three of them, he told himself, to try again.

He heard Nennius' music roaring up from the office even before he let himself into the house. It was a record which he had come to know well over the past weeks, songs from a simpler time, when Nennius had been a husband and a father with a future, not a shell-shocked heap of a man already partly dead.

The music was so loud inside the house that Quinn didn't immediately notice that the phone was ringing. He picked up the receiver in the hall. 'Hello,' he said, protecting his free ear from the tumult down below.

'Success!' a man's voice exploded at him. 'I've been ringing all evening. Might I speak with David?'

'Who is this, please?' shouted Quinn, reaching for the pad on which he had been noting down Nennius' calls since Sunday.

The man said his name in a way that implied that Quinn should have guessed it: 'Meredith.'

Quinn put down the pad. He sank on to the seat and put his hand to his forehead. 'I'm sorry,' he said, his eyes closed tight, 'David can't talk to you.'

Meredith took a deep breath. 'Look, son,' he sighed. 'What did you say your name was?'

Quinn hesitated, then told him.

'Look, Quinn. Couldn't you just ask David to come to the phone, just so that —'

But at that point Quinn, still dutiful, replaced his receiver.

The music pounded on. Quinn stood. On the wall above the

phone was a framed picture which Quinn had always liked: a reproduction of an old Western Region rail advert. There was a sunny view of a wide tree-lined street which led down to a church. Underneath, it said *Royal Leamington Spa* and, beneath that again, *Travel by Train*.

Meredith, Quinn thought as he stared at the picture, Meredith. . . . Several days after Meredith's call on New Year's Day, Quinn had remembered why the name had sounded familiar. Someone called Meredith had once lived in the house.

Quinn had seen the name on letters, mainly circulars, which arrived from time to time with Nennius' own mail. Usually Nennius threw these letters away. Occasionally he would open the envelopes, look briefly at their contents, and then, Quinn presumed, forward them to the former occupant's new address. A number of Meredith's books were still in the house, too, down in the office. Quinn had seen his name inscribed on their title pages.

He picked up the biro which lay beside the pad and drew its cool point along his thumb. Perhaps Meredith just wanted his books back now. In different circumstances, Quinn might have asked Nennius why he wanted nothing to do with this man.

But Meredith really wasn't Quinn's problem. Quinn's problem was sitting downstairs inside his maelstrom of noise. And, with or without the help of the girl at the Samaritans, Quinn had to go on handling it as best he could.

For another week Nennius spent almost all his time in the office, drinking, waiting, tapping at his keyboard with a kind of grimace on his face – a look, Quinn thought, that seemed close to disgust. He went out only to buy cigarettes and whisky from the off-licence. And Quinn always followed him.

Then, shortly before ten on the next Wednesday evening, Nennius left the house in great haste and returned to the Samaritans Centre.

8

Quinn's visit to the Centre had bothered Rachel. His harrowed black-eyed face had stayed with her. In the technical sense she had dealt with him quite properly. She knew that. But still she felt frustrated.

Apart from anything else, she would have welcomed additional information on David Nennius. She believed that Quinn really had come to see her about the other man (although that hadn't stopped her from making out file cards on him, too). But from their talk she had learned only that Nennius was an electrician, which surprised her a little, and that he had a connection with Quinn, which surprised her rather more.

On the next Wednesday evening, she anticipated that either Nennius or Quinn would come back to the Centre. When neither of them did, she felt crestfallen. She believed that she had let both clients down. And, although she was unable to do anything practical, she spent much of the evening speculating about the nature of their relationship.

The obvious thought was that homosexuality was involved. Up to a point, Quinn had been behaving like a scorned lover, his jitteriness contrasting markedly with Nennius' rather majestic brooding stillness. Yet the purely homosexual angle didn't satisfy Rachel. She couldn't say why. It just seemed inadequate – partly because the two men seemed so ill-matched and partly, she knew, because she *wanted* it to be inadequate.

Alasdair, off duty the previous week, was again the leader on the third Wednesday of the New Year. When Rachel phoned in at the end of her shift, he brought up the matter of Nennius.

'There *was* a Melissa,' he said. 'One or two of the others

remembered her. A black girl. She seems to have gone right out of circulation, though. She's not much use to us now, I'm afraid.'

'Oh dear,' said Rachel, giving no hint that she had already heard as much from Grace. 'To be honest, I'm feeling bad about that whole thing. I think I should have got more out of David Nennius.'

Alasdair laughed softly. 'Rachel, you can only listen. If the client wants you to know something, he'll tell you in his own good time. You can't rush these things. But you know that as well as I do by now.'

'Yes,' she said, shaking her head. 'Yes.' Then she invited Alasdair and Maggie to dinner on Saturday week.

She was inviting them only after a long and difficult discussion with Matthew. At first he had been adamant that they shouldn't come. Rachel was quite aware that he'd been avoiding Alasdair on purpose, on account of his own embarrassment at failing to land a 'serious' new job. In the end, however, she had persuaded him to relent.

'By the way,' Alasdair told her before ringing off, 'I did ask Maggie if there was a historian called Nennius. And I was right.'

'Oh, really.'

'Yes. Around AD 800. A Welsh scholar. Apparently he put together a mish-mash of myths and legends and bits of history, and then called the whole thing "a heap"!'

'Well, there you are, then,' laughed Rachel, and they said goodbye.

It had been a chastening evening, and there wasn't any immediate prospect of improvement. After talking to Alasdair, Rachel had to wait until ten-fifteen, a quarter of an hour after her shift was due to end, before her successor showed up. When she got outside it was raining hard.

As she bent to align the combination on her bicycle lock she heard a man's footsteps, approaching from around the corner. She guessed who it was before he said hello to her.

'David,' she said, straightening up and smiling.

He was wearing the same fawn overcoat, blue tracksuit and yellow fingerless mittens. The plaster had gone from his forehead, to reveal a short dark scab. In the dimness of the front garden he seemed less monumental than when he'd been inside the Centre. He also looked dreadfully tired.

Rachel wished that he could have turned up half an hour earlier. She wondered how best to explain to him that she was off duty, and that if he wanted help he would now have to find a phone and call her successor, who had locked himself inside the Centre for the night.

'I'm actually on my way home,' she said. 'But if you'd like to speak with someone. . . .'

'Might I buy you a drink?' Nennius asked her with a gentle smile.

'Oh,' said Rachel. 'Oh, now, I really don't. . . .'

'Just down the road there?'

Rachel smiled, flushed and shook her head. 'It's a lovely idea, David,' she said. 'But I've got to get home. To my husband. I'm already late as it is.' She looked down, hating herself for having brought in Matthew, hating herself for having been so unprofessional.

'There's a phone there,' Nennius said quite evenly.

'Sorry?'

'In the pub, there's a phone. You could give your husband a call. Tell him there's no need for him to worry. I'd just like to buy you a drink. And talk, if you'd let me.' He indicated the building behind him and shrugged. 'I can't talk in there.'

Rachel closed her eyes. She was so late. She could see Matthew pacing his study, then slamming the front door, revving up the car and cruising the roads to the Centre, eyes peeled for signs of misadventure. And already she was thinking that a phone call would put *his* mind at ease.

She bent down again and unlocked her bicycle. The rain was dripping from the hood of her coat.

Consorting with clients outside the Centre was frowned upon. It gave the client a degree of expectation which it was unwise, possibly even dangerous, to foster. In twenty months as a Samaritan, Rachel had never considered doing it before. She thought of Matthew, then of Alasdair, then of Quinn, and then of this towering man at her side. But, finally, she thought of herself.

'I'll ride on ahead and make my call,' she said, standing. 'I'll meet you inside. It'll have to be just one drink, though.'

He nodded. Rachel mounted her bicycle, pulled her skirt tight over her knees, and rode five hundred yards down the road to the pub just off the roundabout. As she rode she looked around, in vain, for Quinn.

A darts match was going on in a saloon bar cloudy with cigarette smoke. Rachel passed through and found a payphone in the corridor, between the toilet doors.

'Matthew,' she whispered as soon as her husband answered. 'Darling. I'm going to be a little later tonight. I've got a client on the other line and we've been talking for forty minutes. It can't go on for much longer now. As soon as he hangs up I'll be out of the building.'

'Would you like me to come and pick you up?' Matthew asked at once. 'I could put your bike in the boot.'

'No, no, I'll be fine. Honestly. I'll see you very soon.'

She replaced the receiver and hung her head. She didn't like lying to Matthew. But gradually, and never for her own benefit, she had got into the habit – whenever the truth just wasn't good enough for him.

She looked up and saw Nennius standing in the doorway to the lounge bar, a banknote folded between his huge fingers. 'What will you have?' he asked.

The lounge smelt of fried onions and damp. Rachel took off her coat, sat, and laid it beside her on the seat while Nennius fetched an orange juice and a whisky. She had gone to the Centre straight from work, and was wearing her black two-piece suit and high heels. Two old couples were sitting at the only other occupied table. One of the women smiled at her.

'Your hair looks nice down,' said Nennius, sitting. He kept his coat on.

'Thank you,' said Rachel without smiling. She tried to tell herself that she wasn't on duty now, that the normal rules didn't apply. So she took the initiative and asked him directly: 'How have you been?'

In the other bar there was a tremendous round of shouting from the darts match. Nennius thoughtfully set down his glass on the table-top. He took a cigarette from his packet without offering one to Rachel. He had to lean backwards and sideways to ask one of the old men for a light. And when he turned again to Rachel she saw in his tired eyes a fearful look that made her think at once of Quinn.

That look made her dismiss any lingering idea that Nennius was dangerous. He might have been dangerous once, but not any longer. She just wished that she could look inside his muddled patrician head and see what was making him dangerous only to himself. She noticed that his gaze had dropped to the wedding ring on her left hand.

'You're probably happily married,' Nennius said softly. 'I hope you are.' He looked across at the bar. 'I was happy once, for a while, with Melissa – and the boy.' He smiled. 'But I married the wrong woman, Rachel. That was what I did wrong. And I paid for it. I'm still paying. Because there has only, ever, been one woman for me. And soon now I'll be going to her.'

Rachel leaned forward. She didn't want the old people to hear, although they weren't obviously eavesdropping. 'This woman,' she said. 'Please tell me about her, David. You see, I don't understand: if you go to her, why do you have to die?'

Nennius balanced his cigarette on the rim of the ashtray. He drank some whisky, then sat up straight and clamped his hands on to his thighs. 'You have to believe', he began, 'that I'm not holding anything back on purpose.' Then he smiled, in wholly believable vexation, and fell silent.

'Tell me this, then,' said Rachel. 'Is the other woman going to kill you because you married Melissa, and not her?'

Nennius looked down. He was shaking his head, slowly but almost irritably, as if something inside wouldn't settle into its rightful place. 'It's no better in here than it was in that room up the road,' he said finally. 'I can't say it. Any of it.'

One of the old women looked across, then quickly glanced away when Rachel caught her eye. 'If you could say it,' Rachel asked immediately, without giving the question much thought, 'how much difference would that make?'

'I just can't say it,' he told her again. 'Not in these words, not in this kind of conversation.' He finished his whisky and stood. Rachel stood, too. When he offered his hand, she shook it.

'I'm sorry to have troubled you again,' he said. 'Give my apologies to your husband. I won't bother you again now. You've been very good. Thank you.' He turned and left the bar, allowing the door to bang shut behind him.

Rachel sat down again and sipped her orange juice. She could have used a stronger drink, but she couldn't let Matthew smell alcohol on her breath when she got home. Matthew: now she had to face Matthew. She looked at her watch and pulled on her coat. The old people said good night to her as she left.

Out in the road, through the rain, she saw Nennius turning into the cul-de-sac in which he had parked his van. Again Rachel looked around for a motorcyclist. Again she saw no one. She fetched her bicycle from the side-alley, then pedalled back home incautiously fast.

She saw as she approached the flat that the curtains in Matthew's study were still open. Behind the window he was typing by the light of a single overhead lamp. He was staring out into the road, but didn't see her as she passed, even though she waved.

She wheeled her bicycle into the garage, then went straight to the study. Unusually, there was no music playing. 'Hello,' she said to Matthew's slim back, his shock of wavy blond hair. 'Home at last.'

Matthew didn't turn. Continuing to stare out of the window, he said in his most formal, least certain voice: 'I tried to call you straight back at the Centre, to say that I'd come and pick you up after all, because of the rain. But they told me you'd left some time before.'

Rachel leaned heavily against the door-frame. Water dripped from her coat on to the carpet. What she really wanted to say to him was: How dare you ring me at the Centre? How dare you, when I've made it so clear, so often, that you must call me there only when you absolutely have to? But she saw his concern for her in the hunch of his shoulders. She saw, beyond her own annoyance, that he did love her, at least in part, unselfishly.

She stepped forward, put her arms around his neck, and kissed his temple. Surprisingly, he stiffened. 'I told you a lie', she said, 'because I didn't want you to worry. I was waylaid by a client. I had a quick drink with him. I couldn't really get out of it.'

'And then he followed you home?' said Matthew.

Rachel drew back, her hands still resting on his shoulders. 'What do you mean?'

'Down there,' Matthew said, pointing. 'On the bike. He was crawling up the road after you. He's been waiting out there ever since you came in.'

Rachel peered out in time to see a motorcyclist kick-start his machine, turn round in the road, then ride off.

His crash-helmet was the right colour. His build was about right, too. His pony-tail stood out against the yellowish-white fur collar of his jacket. It was Quinn.

9

'I can't *say* it!' Nennius murmured when he was back inside his van, away from Rachel. He struck the steering-wheel with his fist. He felt furious with himself for even having tried to say it. No girl, however well-meaning, could help him now. For ten years no girl had come close. There was only one woman for him. There had only ever been one.

He shot the van towards the neck of the cul-de-sac, turned past the Centre and headed up the road. As he came out of the long curve he realised that Quinn was no longer in tow.

He had known for weeks that Quinn had been tailing him. He had known but said nothing. Too late, he had realised how important he had become to Quinn, and he didn't have the words to put him straight. That was why – although he saw the truth of this only after the event – he had involved him in those moments of aberration in the roadside lavatory. It was as if he had wanted the foulness of that evening to do his talking for him: 'This is what I am. This is what I've done. Only worse. Much worse.'

He looked again in his mirror. Quinn had followed him to the Centre, and probably as far as the pub. But he wasn't behind the van now. Nennius rubbed his temple, praying that at last Quinn had decided to give up on him.

Almost unconsciously, he had been following the back-street route to Melissa's old home.

When he turned into the narrow little street, his windscreen-wipers were working at their highest speed to cope with the rain. The street was, as always, fully double-parked. He came face to face with a Metro, and the smaller vehicle had to back up for a good thirty yards to let him through. Those thirty yards took him past the house.

When it had been put up for sale, the estate agent had called it an artisan's cottage. But it was no more than a terraced house, with two windows upstairs, one window down, and a door which gave directly on to the street. There were no lights at any of the windows, just an orange glow behind the dimpled oval pane of glass in the front door.

There was no point in stopping, knocking, waiting on the pavement. Melissa wasn't there. She wasn't in the house, the town, or even this part of the country. Melissa and the boy. His boy, their boy. And it was only at the worst of times, when the despair burst inside him like an abscess, that Nennius believed her still to be around.

He drove on, unable to see what he was passing to left and right, but registering none the less the small fenced playing-field, the entrance to the ironworks, the convent behind its wall, the row of mostly boarded shops. Then he turned into a bumpier road, no more than a track. He travelled on down through the deepening darkness, past a single lamp marking the municipal dumping-ground, on to the barred gate of the allotments, at the edge of the flooded frozen meadow.

He left the engine running, lit a cigarette, and switched on the radio. The manager of a football club was being interviewed. Nennius listened, staring ahead at the gate. He closed his eyes.

At once the lips were large before him, the space between them widening as they twisted: moaning, gasping, spitting up blood charged with gobbets of phlegm, mewling, weeping, a *man's* mouth. And then suddenly the lips were hers, damp and full, opening for him, preparing to call his name. And he felt his penis quicken as he sensed all the love that was waiting, here, only here, where he would dance at the inexpressible end.

He opened his eyes, and the exhilaration faded.

Through the rain-screened darkness, he could scarcely see the allotment area. Allotment number twenty-one was fifty yards to the left: a parcel of land, a high heap of compost, a wooden toolshed with a corrugated-iron roof – the shed in which, almost fifteen months before, he had discovered the vagrant Quinn and briefly, impossibly, mistaken him for someone quite different.

The allotment had been in Nennius' family for thirty-five years. For the last ten years Nennius, once an enthusiastic gardener, had done nothing but stare at it. He stared at it often – by day, by night, sometimes even while Quinn made his occasional attempts to bring the land back into cultivation. Staring was as much as he could do. Staring, he sometimes thought, would have been enough for any man who knew this place of death and discovery for what it was.

He took two last draws on his cigarette, wound down the window and threw out the stub. As soon as he switched off the radio, he felt the shifting beneath him, and he heard her.

I know you, she purred at him, her shocking half-masculine voice as close to derision as it had ever come. *I know you, I have found you and I will not let you go.*

'Yes,' Nennius replied, nodding, as he backed up and turned the van. 'I know.'

He did know. He knew it so completely that he wasn't even sure if he was still afraid. He just longed for it to be over. But he knew what was still required of him. He knew that nothing could happen until he had tied up all the loose ends back in his office.

He nosed his way with care down on to the truer roads, then drove up the hill to a public lavatory on the perimeter of an unfenced park. Again he drew up, but this time he switched off the engine and climbed out into the teeming rain.

It was extremely dark. The houses opposite were set well back from the road, at the end of winding drives, behind hedges. The lavatory itself was much larger than the one to which Quinn had driven him. Brick-built and almost abutting on the pavement, it stood outside the range of the beam cast by the nearest street-lamp. Nennius turned up his overcoat collar. Then he walked towards the open doorway in the building's right flank.

This was the place. Here, just over ten years ago, he had reached the end before the end.

The soles of his training-shoes flapped against the wet tiles of the entrance corridor. He turned the corner to face five gleaming white urinals. To his right were the three cubicles.

It was brighter in there than he remembered. The graffiti on the walls and cubicle doors, which had made the place so fearsome ten years before, had long since been scrubbed away. The condom-dispenser near the sink was new, as was the mirror and the hot-air hand-drier.

It had become a clean respectable place. A place for men on the road to stop off and spruce themselves up. Nennius breathed deep and, again, all he could do was stare. He could see nothing, smell nothing, feel nothing. This whole place – or, rather, the place that it had been in those few minutes that had mutilated his life – belonged to the tragic irretrievable past. There was nothing here for him now. Even the echoes no longer sounded.

He turned and walked briskly away. A man in a car-coat came into the corridor as Nennius re-entered the night. 'This bloody rain!' the man laughed, looking up into Nennius' face. Nennius smiled back, trotted to his van with his head down, and drove straight home.

Quinn's motorbike was in the shed. There was a light at his bedroom window.

Behind the window Quinn lay on his bed, wearing the sodden biking gear in which he had followed Rachel to her home.

He heard Nennius coming into the house and switching on the kitchen light. He knew what sound he would hear next: the click of the drinks-cabinet door, before Nennius rummaged for a fresh bottle of whisky. And Nennius wouldn't be disappointed. Quinn had been to the supermarket that afternoon, just as he'd been there every second Wednesday afternoon for fifteen months.

I don't let him down often, Quinn thought, seething. Not often.

He listened to Nennius descend into the basement. The mighty grounded eagle, who battered drunks in public lavatories. Quinn pictured him hunched over his keyboard, surrounded by his shelves of books and records, setting himself to type out more letters. (So many letters now! Who had he found to write so many letters to?) And within moments the music forced its way up both flights of stairs. Quinn almost grinned. It was that same old record.

The first song began tunefully before the drums crashed in, followed by the singer's rasping voice. Quinn closed his eyes. He was thinking of Rachel, of the shameful way he had loitered behind her across town. It would have been so much easier to have drawn alongside, waved her down, and asked again in all humility for her help. He couldn't understand why he had funked it. For nothing could have been as ruinous as losing Nennius. Nothing. And on his own, minute by minute, it was clear that he was losing the big man. In many of the ways that mattered, he had lost him already.

He turned over and lay for half an hour with his face buried in the pillow. Although it was late, the music surged on. Whenever the side stopped playing, it paused, gathered its strength, then started to play itself all over again.

At one point the phone rang. It rang and rang. Quinn wasn't prepared to answer it. At that time of night, it could only have been Meredith. And over the past few days Quinn had grown tired of putting down the phone on Meredith. He had even grown tired of wondering what it was that Meredith wanted.

In the silence between two songs, he flung himself over on to his back. Down in the office, he could hear Nennius printing out pages. Quinn's face was full of uncried tears. The world around him had narrowed to the width of his room, his bed, his own hollowed-out carcass. Only silence remained.

The next song began. A gentle acoustic guitar, then the singer's voice, distant yet at the same time winding itself all around Quinn – with a lament for a bad, sad, blue-eyed man who was fated to live a life of lies.

Quinn felt as if something had fallen to pieces inside his chest. He was certain, now, that he was reaching an end. After little more than a year, he was right back where he had started.

As the song gathered its momentum, he turned on to his side and crossed his wrists beneath his chin. He knew that if he allowed himself to cry now he would find it very hard to stop. But thankfully, soon after the song finished, he drifted off to sleep.

At three in the morning he woke with a start.

The house was thick with quiet. He left his room at once. Out on the landing he heard Nennius snoring in his room. But downstairs the kitchen light was still on. Quinn went down to switch it off. In the hall he noticed that a soft light was coming from the basement.

He descended the second stairway, crossed the dark workshop and stepped into the glass-roofed office extension, where a single lamp still burned. The hi-fi lights were showing, too. Quinn switched the system off at the mains, then picked up the full ashtray and tipped its contents into the metal waste-bin. Carefully he scoured out the last of the debris with his finger. As he did so, he noticed that the phone had been reconnected.

While Nennius had been virtually living in the office, Quinn hadn't been in to dust and polish. It was a tiny room, with scarcely enough space for the desk, chair, hi-fi, and small library of books and records. It reeked now of alcohol, stale smoke and sweat.

Straightening up, Quinn noticed something new. Two of the walls had printed pages pinned to them. On most of these pages sections had been underlined in biro, or highlighted with crosses in their margins. Stepping closer, he realised, from the raggedness of their edges, that they had been ripped from the stack of books on the desk. Quinn felt shocked. He was no book-lover, but he believed that they shouldn't be vandalised. He peered at the page just in front of him, on which Nennius had underlined this passage:

> Many people have felt instinctively that there is something 'special' about the Island of Britain; that there may be something in William Blake's claim in his *Jerusalem* that 'All things Begin and End in Albions Ancient Druid Rocky Shore'.

Quinn looked down. Next to the books on the desk was a pile of papers: the letters which he had heard Nennius printing out earlier that night.

Quinn glanced at the top page of the pile. It had no

address or date at the top, and wasn't set out in the manner of one of Nennius' estimates. He stepped closer, and read the entire brief first paragraph.

David Victor Nennius never knew his father. He never even knew his father's name.

Quinn picked up the page.

As a child, he would ask his mother about the man he had never seen. Her answers were terse and sometimes contradictory. She always insisted that the boy's father was no longer alive. . . .

Quinn sat down heavily in Nennius' chair.

He flicked through the pile of unnumbered pages on the desk. There were about forty of them.

He drew up the chair and started to read.

David's Story

1

David Victor Nennius never knew his father. He never even knew his father's name.

As a child he would ask his mother about the man he had never seen. Her answers were terse and sometimes contradictory. She always insisted that the boy's father was no longer alive, that he had been killed in an accident.

David's mother was called Mary. Her maiden name was Machin, and at the time of the boy's conception she had been twenty-eight years old. Most people regarded her as bookish, dried-up, rather pathetic. On the surface of things this was a reasonable enough assessment.

Ten years earlier she had won a place at a northern university to study history. Before the end of the first term, to the enormous disappointment of her academic family, she had given up the course. She had then moved back to her native city in the south. But in the years of world warfare that followed she had joined the services and gradually estranged herself from her parents.

When her father and then her mother died, she attended neither funeral. She refused to accept the small amounts of money which they left her. After her demobilisation, she took a series of typing and secretarial jobs, making just enough money to pay the rent on a basement room close to the city's largest railway station.

A man was waiting inside her room when she came home from work. It was a bright April evening after a period of rain. Blossom from the cherry tree on the pavement was sticking to her damp window-sill and doorstep.

Mary never worked out exactly how the intruder had got in. He took her arm from behind, quite gently, as soon as she shut the door.

This is a beginning, he said. It isn't an end. (His voice was rich, deep, and utterly unfamiliar.)

She closed her eyes. The shock of his first touch numbed her to all that came afterwards. But, numbed as she was, she remained keenly aware of everything that was happening both to her and around her. It was as if the hideous fact of his presence was shedding its own brilliant light.

Still behind her, unseen by her, the man peeled off her raincoat, then the jacket of her two-piece.

I don't intend to hurt you, he said.

Something powerful inside Mary prevented her from screaming. It was something she couldn't reason with. She felt the stiffness going out of her body. She bowed her head.

What must I do? she asked quietly.

He wheeled her round until she faced him. Her head was still bowed, and she didn't dare to open her eyes and look at him. He had an unlikely smell, resinous, almost sweet. She listened to the ticking of her alarm-clock. Up above in the street a boy was passing by, bouncing a ball.

He drew her to him, pressing her head against his collarbone, and Mary opened her eyes with a start when she realised that he was naked. But, crushed up against him, all she could see was her bed, her books, her sink, her mirror. And then she felt her limp arms rising to return his embrace.

I'm a virgin, she said, knowing how wrong it was to tell him.

He maintained his hold on her but didn't reply for some moments.

Do you prize your virginity? he said at last.

Mary tried to stop her thoughts from wandering, to the street above, to the slowing of the trains, to the dark gold stain in her sink. She sensed from his touch that he was a practised man – the sort of man whom she herself had wanted, in the days before she had dissuaded herself from wanting anyone at all.

He repeated his question. Do you prize your virginity?

She couldn't answer.

Take off your things, he said. I want you. I'm here for you.

She closed the curtains. Then, with her back to him, she removed all her clothes. It was only when she turned that she dared to look into his face.

He could have had any girl. He had no need to be breaking into basements. He belonged on the world's higher floors.

He reached out, and she allowed him to take her by the hand.

Why do you want me? she asked. Why me?

He smiled, and even through her temporary paralysis she was afraid of that smile, because there was weakness behind it.

He pulled her to him. He kissed her on her mouth and then inside it. There were footsteps in the room above. But Mary closed her eyes again, and she heard nothing but the drumming inside her own head.

He lifted her on to the bed, held her thighs, and worked at her with his tongue. She had started to cry, passively, almost calmly. When the first tears appeared in the corners of her eyes, he raised his head and gently licked them away.

Mary had been naked with men before. She had held a man's penis in her hand. Men had even kissed her in these parts of her body. But when she stopped sobbing he reared up and, as no man had ever done before, he eased himself inside her.

She gasped, but that was all. He was indeed a practised man. Somewhere close by, a telephone was ringing. The footsteps continued overhead. Mary opened and closed her eyes, opened and closed her eyes, and she began to believe that this could go on for ever.

The expression on her assailant's face was indeterminate. There was nothing about him that Mary hated, least of all the fearful weakness in his smile.

She felt, very soon, that she had known him all along, that they had been lifelong partners. She felt that as a couple they were so old, so experienced in their loving, that what they were doing had become no more than an act of reassurance. She didn't respond to his movement. But in her mind she was with him.

You're mine, he said to her just before he spent himself. There was neither warmth nor menace in the way that he said it.

Beyond the door and the curtained window the evening was still very bright. Mary turned on to her side and cried again. She wasn't a part of a couple after all. She wasn't old but unbearably young. Then, and only then, it was in her to scream. But she tensed herself instead, and waited for the end.

She didn't look back to watch him dress. She didn't see the going of him. But before he went he came to her bedside and put his hand on her shoulder.

This isn't an end, he said once again.

There was no answer for her to give, lying there on her side, fresh from the gaining and the losing of it all. All she could do was continue to cry, beneath the click of the closing of her door, the ticking of her clock, the heaving of the trains. But she knew, even then, that for better or for worse he had been right.

This had been a beginning.

Six weeks later she learned that she was pregnant. And by that time Mary Machin had already decided what she was going to do.

2

Mary Machin told no one about what had happened to her.

These were narrow times in the island. Mary knew that she could expect little sympathy, but she had no deep wish to diminish her secret by sharing it. Instead she severed every thread connecting her with her own past.

She took out her savings, packed some cases, then travelled by a sequence of trains into the north of the island. The further she travelled the younger she felt. The land itself seemed to be losing its age with her. Not just years, but decades, centuries. And as it lost its age, so it lost its familiarity.

Mary stared out at the crowded stations, at the swaths of smoke and relentless brickwork – and she registered none of it. What she was seeing, what she was feeling, was something far more ancient. In her heart she was crossing a different island, dark and silent and hungry. She was crossing the land that lay *within* the island which she had always known – a land whose secret was related, in some indefinable way, to her own.

The town she chose to stay in lay just to the south of the high Roman Wall. There was a young women's hostel for her to sleep in until she found a more suitable home. There were any number of offices where she would be able to earn her living.

She played havoc with her appearance, bought herself a wedding ring, invented a dead husband, and changed her surname from Machin to Nennius.

She borrowed the new name, in a spirited rush of self-mockery, from the spine of one of her books. The original Nennius, a ninth-century Welsh monk, had compiled one of the island's earliest histories. *The scholars of the island of Britain had no skill*, he had written in his preface, *and set down no record in books. I have therefore made a heap of all that I have found. . . .*

Eventually she found what she was looking for: a tiny one-storey cottage to rent, in a village outside the town. Its ceiling sloped, but it was dry. And there were just enough neighbours on hand to help her when the time for help would come.

By day she then worked as a clerical officer at an inspectorate in town. At night she would make clothes. But the child inside her grew quickly, and by October she was finding the daily bus journeys to and from the town unendurable.

Her colleagues said goodbye to her with gifts. If any of them had ever doubted her tale of a dead husband, not one of them had said so for her to hear. It was the same with the handful of people in her village. They wanted to believe the best about her. They wanted her to have experienced a tragedy which left no stigma.

During the weeks that followed Mary read a great deal – history-books for the most part, lives of the island's great politicians and poets, men whose legends had been layered into the land itself.

Since childhood she had preferred to approach her history from the angle of the individual. She had always believed that the truth could be found within one man, one woman. Years before, she had tried to explain this to her university tutors. They had listened with barely concealed contempt. They had found her, she realised, quite juvenile. They hadn't even argued when she had told them soon afterwards that she was intending to leave.

There was no one in the village with whom she could talk about such things. But there was a schoolboy, who began by bringing Mary cakes and puddings from his mother, and ended by accompanying her on short afternoon walks alongside a towering stretch of the Wall. The boy's name was William. He was handsome, well built, thoughtful and sometimes moody.

What do they teach you about the Wall at school? Mary asked him on one of their walks. There were scatters of snow on the ground, and it was sorrowfully cold.

At first he simply shrugged. They walked on, Mary looking up, William looking down. But as they neared the village again he said to her: In the old times, the people south of the Wall believed that only the dead lived to the north of it.

Mary slowed down. When William turned to her, she frowned at him but said nothing. Then they continued on their way.

Before they parted outside Mary's cottage, William spoke again. What are you going to call your son? he asked, kicking a loose stone off the path.

Mary smiled. How do you know it's going to be a boy?

If it is, though. What will you call him?

Mary smiled. Alone in her cottage at nights she had been listing the possibilities. A king's name, she said at last. I'll name him after a king.

A king of England? Like me?

No, I don't think so, she told him. A king of Scotland perhaps. Or of Israel.

William pulled an extravagant face for Mary to see. She laughed, and pushed him away from her.

In the days that followed, Mary often looked to the north from her window. William's recounting of the old belief had troubled her. It had made her feel, again, that there was not just one island but two, the second within the first – and that one was for the living while one was for the dead.

When the mobile library next came to the village, she took out a book of travellers' tales about the island, chronologically arranged.

Only its introduction was of interest to Mary. She found a record of what William had told her. The area to the north of the Wall had indeed once been seen as the home of departed spirits. But there was more.

An eastern historian reported the belief that the entire island was a rendezvous for the souls of the dead.

He told of certain men, dwellers on the northern coast of France. In the middle of the night, these men would hear a knocking at their doors, and a low voice calling them. Then an unknown force would draw them down to the sea, where they always found boats waiting. And, although the boats seemed quite empty, they were clearly bearing loads, for their gunwales never rose by more than a finger's breadth above the waters.

The task entrusted to the men – a task which since time immemorial had freed them from paying all tribute to their rulers – was to row the invisible cargoes across to the island's rocky shores.

But, whereas in their own boats this crossing would take them a day and a night, in these heavy boats it took but one hour, and the island at its end was not as they knew it. They never saw a person on its shore, but they heard a voice, reciting names. And when at last silence fell the boats would be high in the water, for the voice had been counting ashore the rowers' unseen passengers – the souls of the world's dead, arriving at the place where all things must end.

Mary read this account many times.

At length she closed the book and balanced it on the arm of her fireside chair. The account had intrigued her and unsettled her, but it failed to satisfy her stronger curiosity.

Something, her instinct told her, had been missing from it, something important, something – and this notion seemed irrefutable – *feminine*.

She sensed that all those who had ever come to this ancient inner island had come on account of a *woman*. She was convinced that the voice, which had been calling the roll of the dead since the beginning of time, had been a woman's voice.

Bewildered, she began to doze.

Minutes later she opened her eyes with a start and sat forward in her chair. It seemed that the older island was flexing itself beneath her. It seemed to be assuring her that it was as womanly as she was herself. Mary stiffened as the ground lurched again, and she smiled a petrified smile. She believed that she was beginning to understand. But in truth she had gone into labour, two months before her baby's due date.

3

Mary waited for the first contractions to pass. Then she eased herself out of her chair and shuffled across to the front door. It was just after noon on the last day of October. The sun stood cold and high above the village.

The boy William was at his front gate, absorbed in conversation with a friend. He saw how Mary was holding herself and began to run towards her.

Fetch your mother, she shouted, waving him back. I'm having my baby.

She went inside the cottage. The contractions began again as soon as she sank into her chair. She knew it was happening too quickly. Too quickly and too soon. William's mother appeared in the doorway with the boy behind her. She looked at Mary and she knew at once that it was too late for the hospital. Leaving William behind, she went herself for the midwife.

Mary, breathing faster, saw the alarm in William's face. Would you read to me, please? she said, handing him the book of travellers' tales from the arm of her chair.

William took the book, opened it out on the dining-table and pulled up a chair. His cheeks were bright. Mary closed her eyes and she felt again, as if for the first time, the touch of the man who had sired her child. Momentarily it reassured her. But then she remembered the weakness in his smile, and she felt pure fear.

In a small voice William began to read to her from the book's introduction.

Slowly his reading acquired some rhythm, but Mary could hear none of the words. She wanted to cry and scream and accuse and rant. But William's voice ran on, melodious now, almost portentous. Mary closed her eyes, to sink inside the sound of it.

But beyond his voice stood the silence of the Wall. And all around was the echoing silence of the land which had always received the world's dead, the darker island which spoke with the voice of a woman.

Then Mary saw again the man who had waited in her room, splendid but weak. She knew that the father of her child was close to her now, above her, as close in his way as the woman who lay in constant wait beneath.

William read on. He read of that division of the island which was marked by the Wall. Mary felt the child inside her battling. And she knew the words which William was about to speak. Half of her wanted to stop the words from being spoken. The other half knew that it was only in order to reach them that the boy had been reading at all.

He began to recount the story of the cargo of midnight spirits. Mary opened her eyes and she saw only water, endless expanses of water. Then the water was gone. There was no sea, no land, no sky. She had returned to the beginning, to the time before form. She closed her eyes and still she saw nothing but the emptiness.

Stop! Mary thought to scream at William. Go on! she urged him with the other part of her mind, because in spite of her terror she longed to see more.

The boy continued to read. His words made Mary see. She saw one island in the silent emptiness. The island was a smiling woman, through whose lovely features a hideousness flickered.

From the beauty within herself this island generated first the seas and then the living, unpeopled lands of the earth. And lastly, as a consort for herself, she generated the sheltering sky. The sky drew itself out into the shape of a man. He was a marvellous man, but there was no strength in his smile, and Mary knew his face. . . .

No! she shouted, coming forward in her chair.

William looked up, aghast.

And immediately his mother was beside him, breathless,

explaining that the midwife and doctor were on their way. She told the boy that he could go.

Thank you, Mary called after him, ashamed at having shouted. Yet the knowing of the woman and the man, of the island and the sky, would not leave her. And it was not the fact of the man that was tormenting her. For she had been with that man, and he had already done to her all that he could do.

William's mother helped her into the tiny bedroom. The shadow of a waiting figure was in there. It was the shadow, Mary knew, of the woman.

Oh, don't let the woman take my child, Mary pleaded, beginning to weep.

William's mother helped her on to the bed, and started to undress her, laughing. She thought that Mary had meant the midwife.

Mary felt the lurching inside her, the impatience and the strength. But she was no longer marking the course of her own labour. Instead, astounded, she was following the sequence of images in her mind. Now she was seeing it all.

First she saw the man upon the woman, sky upon island: their ceaseless, ever more frantic coupling, as they sought to beget the race of immortals that would inhabit the earth. But then the man withdrew, leaving the woman bereft. For her labours of creation had used her up: she had become barren, and her own wide earth remained unpeopled.

Then Mary saw the man again, procreating, effortlessly, with the living lands of the eastern world. The lands bore countless children. And the woman of the island learned of these children fathered by the sky. She was covetous of them, and in her covetousness she conferred upon them mortality. She allowed them to beget children of their own, but then she called into her western fastness all the sons and daughters of the sky. And there she created for them, out of the hideousness inside herself, the place where all things have their end. Through her, the children of the sky passed into that dark place. Through her, every mortal man and woman until the end of time would pass into this dark place after death. This place was known to her as Albion.

You're coming along fast, said a voice new to Mary, the voice of the midwife. It won't be long now.

And at last Mary saw what had happened to herself. She saw, infrequently through the ages, the incontinent sky taking again the form of man. He would mate with the children of his own children. And the unforgiving island woman would summon the sons thus begotten while still in their prime.

In her vindictiveness she would call these new sons of the sky westward. And, at the gateway to Albion, she would make them perform, in that brightest light which sits for ever upon the darkness, the dance of death. . . .

Mary gripped the bedhead. All she knew now was the midwife, and the midwife's soothing voice. She wanted, badly, to confide in the midwife, to tell her the truth about herself and her child. But the midwife had no wish to talk, only to issue instructions. Mary's body responded instinctively, without the intercession of her mind. Her mind was too preoccupied. Her mind was lost in the shadow.

Good! Good! Good! the midwife cried. I have the head!

William's mother was next to her, weeping. The head was screaming. A strong scream. This was no feeble early child.

Mary opened her eyes and she saw no shadow, no vindictive woman waiting, none of the truth about herself. Only the ceiling and the wall of a tiny cottage room made warm by the scream of her own strong child.

He's here, said the midwife, holding the bloodied bundle for Mary to take. He's here for you. He's perfect, and he's huge.

Mary took her son. And then she heard the voice, sounding inside her own head, but speaking, she knew, to the child and not to her.

I know you, said the voice of the covetous island, *I know you, I have found you and I will not let you go.*

4

On the morning after the birth William's mother returned to the cottage.

Mary was weeping, with the child asleep at her breast. The words of the island woman were with her still. And so was her need to confide, to confess, to puncture her fear by telling her truth.

I have never been married, she said, looking up.

William's mother came forward. She kissed the child on its smeared black hair. There's no reason to let *him* know that, she replied as she kissed the child again.

Neither woman spoke again before the door opened. It was William, on his way to school. Mary smiled at him. He stepped closer.

So what will you call him? he asked.

David, said Mary. Yes, David.

William nodded. And his second name?

I haven't thought, Mary replied. What do you suggest?

William shrugged. Victor?

Yes, Mary laughed, to disguise more tears. David Victor. It's good.

David Victor Nennius, William's mother said slowly. It is good.

William smiled and left the cottage.

But he came back, often. Sometimes he would nurse the child while Mary took the bus into town to shop. And later, when Mary gave evening classes to supplement her small savings and allowance, William would wash the child and tell him tales before setting him to sleep.

David himself was placid as a baby, increasingly robust as a toddler. His dark hair fell out to be replaced by blond curls. He was big but not yet remarkably bigger than other boys. As soon as he was old enough to talk, he called William 'Daddy', and neither William nor Mary corrected him.

Mary guessed that William was in love with her. She felt flattered. Occasionally she would pretend to herself that he was the boy's true father. It was an easier way to puncture her fear. For, although she was otherwise happy, this fear continued to swell inside her, and she prayed constantly for protection for her child.

But at last, before the boy's fourth birthday, Mary found the mere possibility of protection insufficient. She told William the truth. Sitting in her chair by the fire, she told him of the child's conception. And then, in tears, she described what she had seen and heard at the time of David's birth.

As she spoke, William sat hunched at her table – just as he had hunched himself to read to her from the book of travellers' tales. He was almost sixteen now. His face darkened by the moment.

Mary knew even before she finished that it had been wrong to tell him. She crossed to the table. Then, as if it were he who needed succour, she closed her hand over his. His hand was far bigger than hers. She was more than twice his age. If he tries to kiss me now, she thought, nearer to despair than ever before, I'll let him.

But William only looked at her hand. I want you, he said levelly. I have always wanted you.

Mary tried to laugh. I'm just a ridiculous woman, she said. A madwoman with a child.

William kept his eyes on their heap of hands. I have only wanted you more, he told her, since David came.

Then he rose, touched her shoulder, and left the cottage. Mary poured herself a small glass of whisky. She sat sipping from it, listening to the radio. She had found no consolation in sharing her truth, and she regretted having made William share his. She wanted to open the cottage door and shout after him: Come back! I didn't mean it! *You* didn't mean it! We can go back to before the words!

On the next night William did return. Mary was again in her chair, knitting for David. She could tell that William had been drinking. His eyes seemed too large for his face.

I want to marry you, he began and ended. I want to stop you from being frightened.

Out in the tiny kitchen, a tap was dripping into the sink. William was standing in the middle of the room, his arms poised at his sides. Mary looked across at the dresser, to where the whisky-bottle lay on its side in the bread-bin. Then she looked to the darkness beyond the doorway where David was asleep. Her gaze fell to his little pedal car, the fluff on the mat in front of the fire, the gleaming curve of the coal-scuttle. She put her knitting aside.

Don't you think I'm mad? she said. To be frightened of the things that frighten me?

William raised his arms and held them out to her. Mary saw the activity in his face, the tension at the hinge of his jaw. Why won't you tell me I'm mad, William? she said. Say that it's not true about the woman. Just say it.

William took a step forward. His hands were almost close enough for her to touch. She had begun to cry. Slowly she raised herself. Then she was in his arms, crying hard but silently into his shoulder, lest she should wake the child. She wanted this William, she wanted the wrongness of being pressed against him.

No, she heard herself saying in vain.

And when she put her lips to his cheeks, his nose, his mouth, his eyes, she tasted the salt of her own tears. The shadow, she knew, was around them both. The shadow of the smiling woman, waiting for her moment.

No, she said again. Mary could not stop crying, even as William knelt and made her naked. She felt no shame before him. She felt no shame before the woman. William stood and he was white without his clothes, in front of the flickering fire.

No, Mary said to all who were there to listen, and William entered her while they were still on their feet, pressing her back against the edge of the table.

This was not like the first time. Mary knew that it could

67

only be an end. But she held William tight. The weight went out of her. She wanted this to go on.

For a protracted moment she drew her upper body away. His face was wild with her tears and her lipsticked kisses. This was no beginning. It couldn't be a beginning. She was listening again to the dripping of the tap, thinking of the darkness behind her, of the pedal car, the fluff, the silence of the shadow.

She sobbed against the strong boy's neck and chest, mottled red now with exertion. She could hear the table behind her grinding against the wall. She heard her unwashed dinner things trembling on its surface. And the woman was inside and around it all.

William drove her back for one last, painful time. At last he slid out of her, knelt, and rested his head against her thighs. Mary held her own spinning head in her hands. For a moment there was no sound.

Daddy, a small voice then said from the bedroom doorway.

Both naked figures twisted to see David, sitting on the floor in the darkness, pointing past them, gently rocking back and forth.

5

Mary packed her belongings, then let the villagers know she was leaving. She didn't tell William herself. She had no more words for William. And he, it seemed, had no more for her. But on the night before the departure William's mother came.

Can you really not say why you're going? she asked.

Mary, standing at the table to iron a blouse, shook her head.

Do you have somewhere to go?

Mary nodded. I'm going back to where I came from, she said. It's important to me.

William's mother looked at her. Are you going to the boy's father?

I am, Mary replied in a rush of relief. Yes, I am. Then she burst into tears. And for almost an hour, in response to questioning, she concocted a man for herself. A man whom she loved, a man who had initially let her down over the boy, but who now wanted her as badly as she had always wanted him.

Then when she was alone again she went in to her son.

He was asleep on his back. A great strong-featured boy, with a face that was lengthening like Mary's. A quiet clean child, not given to tantrums. He had not spoken of what he had seen on the night with William. Mary in turn hadn't tried to exonerate herself. It had happened, it had been witnessed. It was too big for lies and too small, at that time, for any kind of truth. But the fact of it was with them always, like a third person, who might one day drive them apart or possibly – if God had any mercy – bring them closer together.

The taxi came before most of the villagers had risen. Mary

and David were the only passengers on the platform at the station. It was a cold hazy morning. The boy sat puffy-eyed on the bench with a pillow-case full of toys beneath his feet. Mary put her arm around him. She loved him. He had asked her no questions which she could not answer.

They were sitting in the train when William stepped on to the platform.

He saw Mary at once and indicated that she should come to the pull-down window. She did as he wished. With the train door between them she searched his expressionless face.

Marry me, he said.

Mary inclined herself towards him and kissed him on the mouth. She wanted to tell him goodbye, but the words would not come. I'm sorry, she said, unsure of whom she was addressing.

A porter called out. The train jerked into motion. William walked along the platform, still abreast of Mary's window. He broke into a trot, staring at her, saying nothing. Mary couldn't take her eyes from his. Just before the train pulled out of the station, he opened his mouth.

Mary would carry away with her that last glimpse of him.

His face seemed to have been distorted by a furious kind of panic. He looked savage, as if he were about to hurl himself bodily against the glass. Mary put a hand to her throat. Then he was gone.

Mary ran her tongue over her lips and closed her eyes. In time she returned to her seat. David was looking up at her, rocking, smiling.

Their tickets took them into the south of the island, to a town which Mary had never visited. Mary had already booked a room in a guest-house that catered mainly for commercial travellers. The two of them stayed there for a month. Then she found a cheap bedsit room in the town's industrial suburb and took part-time work which allowed her to keep the boy by her.

When David started school, Mary settled into a job in the typing pool of a car showroom.

The pay was poor, and she fretted incessantly over the boy's safety while they were apart. The showroom manager, a studious gentleman of fifty named Emrys, was kind to her. He talked to her often of literature, and invited her to borrow books from the shelves behind his desk. The other girls found this amusing; they had previously regarded Emrys as unmanly.

When more than a year had passed, and Christmas was approaching, Mary began to lose heart. She sold her last remaining possessions of value in order to buy presents for the boy. They spent the holiday alone in the room.

On New Year's Eve, Mary drank a glass of sherry and swept the sleeping David up into her arms. He was huge and beautifully hot. She rocked him awake. I'll keep you safe, she murmured when he opened his eyes. You're mine. The woman can't have you. I won't let her. And when she looked up she thought she could see the ceiling moving.

On the day that she returned to the showroom, Emrys called her to his office.

He got to his feet when Mary entered. Looking troubled, running his fingers over his trim moustache, he offered her a chair. Then he asked after the boy, to whom he had told a story at the staff Christmas party. Finally he cleared his throat and asked Mary if she would marry him.

But my son? asked Mary, wanting to smile.

Emrys rummaged among the papers on his desk. His face flushed violently. He could be my son, too, he replied, if you would permit that.

Mary stared at the shelf of paperbacks. She was looking back, not forward – back as far as she could see. Then she nodded, uncrossed her legs, and stood.

She told Emrys the truth about David's conception. She said nothing about the woman, nothing about her fear. When she fell silent, Emrys came from behind his desk and laid his hands gently upon her shoulders.

The wedding took place in a registry office in early February. During the ceremony Emrys and Mary mentioned the word *love* to each other for the first time. The girls from the showroom were waiting outside in the street.

It was raining hard. The photos were taken beneath umbrellas.

Preparing to pose with her husband and son, Mary gazed down at the confetti which had stuck to the pavement. She remembered the man who had been waiting in her basement room. She saw again the swollen face of William as her train pulled out of the station.

It's nearly over, she thought. For me, it's nearly over.

That night, in Emrys's spacious book-lined home next to the cinema, she listened as her husband told her son another story before he slept. She smiled to hear him call the boy his Albion, his splendid little giant. Then she made love for the third time in her life.

And she had been right. For her, to all intents and purposes, it was over.

But for the boy it had hardly begun.

6

On the afternoon that Mary died David was nine years old. Cancer killed her, a cancer of the womb. It had been identified two years before, and kept her bedridden for nine months.

David was at a football match when it happened. He came home and Emrys was sitting by the kitchen table, passing a box of matches from hand to hand. He looked up, and David saw the smile that was missing from his face. Before the doctor came, Emrys took the boy to see his mother.

David cried a little but he didn't like to touch her. Emrys had been preparing him for this, and for what was to come after. Already his place at boarding school had been assured, but first there was the funeral.

It was a small affair on a warm May morning. David wept into Emrys's side as they followed the hearse to the cemetery. Later he stared at the coffin inside the horse-shoe of mourners. When he looked up, beyond the immediate ring and into the middle distance, he thought he saw William: just for a moment, head bowed, his hands clasped in front of him. Then he was gone.

That evening Emrys came to David's room. The whole house smelt of flowers and polish. Emrys, still in his waistcoat and suit trousers, sat on the edge of David's bed. He held a glass of whisky. For a while he was silent.

Your mother's life was never easy, he told the boy at last. Yours will be easier. This is a good time to be young.

David looked at him, the man who still called him his Albion, his own splendid giant. (And he in turn called this beloved man his father, though he didn't have his name.) Again for a moment he thought he could see William, the previous surrogate, standing behind him.

Your true father was killed in a crash, his timid mother had always said in answer to his questions. But sometimes she had fixed the crash before the boy's birth and sometimes after. David had listened, he had wondered, and then he had stopped asking.

Emrys drank some whisky.

It wasn't quite dark in the room. Outside on the street people were quietly queuing for the cinema. David put his hands behind his head. He was large. Although only nine, he looked twice that age, and often he longed to be treated as the child he was.

Emrys eyed the stippled shadows on the far wall, then he drank some more.

I don't know, he admitted to the boy, what more I can say. (He paused lengthily.) In an older time, they would have had stories. (Again he paused.) There would have been storytellers, to take this moment and not let it go.

David locked his fingers tight behind his head, then loosened them. He didn't want to be left on his own. Not yet. Not in this uncertain light.

Emrys set his glass on the floor, leaned forward and heaped his hands on his knee. He looked broken. Would you allow me, he asked David, to tell you an old story? It's a story my father once told me. You carry these things with you.

David nodded. He knew that if he spoke he might cry. Emrys looked at him, and he nodded again. He did want to hear. Not necessarily a story, but he wanted to be with Emrys's voice, with Emrys's words and with the silences in between. He saw the man's jaw quivering before he cleared his throat.

There was once an emperor, he began.

He was emperor of the most wondrous empire in the world. Thirty-two kings waited on him, and he wanted for nothing. One day he took the kings hunting, in the river valley west of his celestial city. Under the midday sun he fell asleep and then he dreamed.

74

He dreamed that he travelled a great way from his city, away from the lands he knew. He came to a coast, and a ship at anchor was waiting for him. It took him across the water to a beautiful island.

He left the ship and crossed the island. He came to a rich fortress. Its door was open to him. He went inside, and two young men were playing at a board, while an older man carved gold pieces for the game. Seated between them was the loveliest woman.

When the emperor saw her he had to look away. She was lustrous. As radiant as the sun which had made him sleep and dream, but her look was also as scorching. She rose to greet him, and they embraced, and then they sat together.

That was all. The noise of the hunt woke the emperor from his dream.

In the next days, he wanted only to sleep, so that he might return to the woman. His people grew restless. He spoke of his dream to them: of the island, and of the woman within it. He told them that his love for this woman, coupled with his fear of her, had crippled him. Only by being with her could he hope to be restored. At once messengers were sent out, east and west around the earth, in search of her.

After many years one party landed on the island. It was the fairest island any of them had seen. They travelled on until they came to the fortress. And there, inside, the scene was just as their lord had described it. They kneeled before the woman whose beauty was too resplendent for their eyes.

Come back with us, they begged her, and be crowned empress.

The woman began to smile. This is where I am, she said, and her voice was all around them, within these rocky shores, where all things begin and all things end.

The messengers, awed, returned to tell the emperor of her answer. He was disturbed but pleased. He gathered his army at once, then led his men across land and water to the island.

The kings who ruled in the island raised armies of their own. But the emperor pressed on, driving the kings into the sea, and finally he came to the fortress with its open door.

Now he was filled with a deeper dread.

For, although so close to the woman, he doubted that he could match her. Yet even before he stepped inside her voice was reaching him. She was taking possession of him, as she had taken so many men before and would take so many again.

I know you, she said and her rich voice was inside him already. You, son of the sky. I know you, I have found you, and I will not let you go.

And, fearful as he was, the emperor went forward, unshackled from all that he had ever been and seen. In the blinding brightness which sat upon the dark, the woman received him. And on that night he performed for her the Dance of Albion.

Emrys fell silent. After several minutes he reached down for his whisky, then drained the glass. David stared at him, his arms aching behind his head. Half of him expected the story to go on, but there was no more for Emrys to tell him. He sensed, without yet understanding why, that Emrys had told him everything that mattered.

I'm so sorry, David, the old man said, standing.

He kissed the boy on his forehead, then squeezed his shoulder. David closed his eyes and heard him draw the curtains before leaving the room. Shortly afterwards, music drifted up from the front room as Emrys tried to lose himself in a radio concert.

David thought with all his strength about the woman in the story. She had been familiar. Four years earlier, David had dreamed of such a woman himself, in a cottage by a Wall, on a night of love and wonder.

On that night he had come to the bedroom doorway, sat down, and watched something finer than he had ever imagined.

And when it was over, behind the spent kneeling form of William, behind the exquisite derangement of his mother's body against the dining-table, he had seen a third figure.

Partially concealed by the others, she was also less substantial than they. David glimpsed her face. A smiling face of scorching beauty, mouthing words directly at him, words which he had been unable, then, to read on her lips.

Sitting on the floor, rocking back and forth, he had reached for her. He had needed to ask the others what she was saying to him. As he tried to speak she was gone; and, when at last he spoke, just one word would come from all the love and wonder inside him: *Daddy*.

David drew his arms from behind his head. He fancied that he could hear Emrys crying to his music downstairs, a strange rasping noise against the melody.

He closed his eyes and made himself think only of the woman at the cottage, whose silent communication he was now at last able to decipher.

I know you, she had said to him, just as she had once said to the emperor: You, son of the sky. I know you, I have found you, and I will not let you go.

7

It was, as Emrys had said, a good time to be young in the island. The sun picked out bright new colours in the old landscapes. After the fashion David let his hair grow past his shoulders. He wore beads and bright clothes. He spent long hours cocooned inside the new music. And, because of the island woman, he fought shy of girls.

Whenever he thought back to the woman, he felt ecstasy. She had terrified him, too, because he sensed that there was a heinous underside to her beauty, and he remembered the vindictiveness at the edge of her smile.

On leaving school he trained as an electrician. Soon he became absorbed by both the theory and the practice of the work. Until the age of twenty-two he lived with Emrys. The older man had retired. He spent his last years reading, talking with David of books which both of them had read, listening to music, cultivating his allotment. And it was at the allotment, early one August evening, that David asked him at last for the truth about his father.

Emrys continued to hoe for a little longer before looking up.

Then he produced a packet of cigarettes from the pocket of his cardigan. He gave one to David, took one for himself, but lit neither.

Your mother was assaulted, he said with great steadiness, looking into David's face. A stranger broke into her room. He raped her and made her pregnant. She never knew his name, David. She never saw him again.

The old man smiled. You had to know it, boy, he said. I've been waiting so long to let you know it.

David stared at Emrys and he seemed crushed with years. It was as if he had been expecting his words to bear immediate fruit, but seen them fall instead on the stoniest ground.

David reached out and took Emrys's trembling hand. They stood together for longer than either man would have thought possible. David knew that they were standing in the shadow of the woman.

One week later, at a wedding reception, David Victor Nennius saw the black girl for the first time.

PART TWO

1

Quinn was a slow reader. Thursday morning had dawned when he finished reading the story for the second time. Upstairs Nennius had risen and was moving about in the bathroom.

Quinn searched for more pages. It seemed impossible that the story should have ended on that last tantalising sentence. But there was nothing on the desk-top, in the desk's two larger drawers, or on the bookshelves. The rest of it – if there was more – was probably stored on one of the word-processor discs, which Quinn had no idea how to use.

He shuffled the pages until all their edges were aligned, then set down the pile exactly where he had found it. He left the office as if in a trance, mounted both flights of stairs, entered his room, locked the door and climbed into bed with his clothes on.

Across the landing Nennius was humming to himself in the shower. Quinn couldn't believe how wrong he had been about the big man. The apparent irrelevance of sex to them both had formed, he thought, an important bond between them. Now Quinn knew that no such bond existed. For there it had been: Nennius' sexual appetite, leaving its glistering trail across each of those peculiar pages.

Quinn heard Nennius leave the bathroom, and simply rolled on to his side. Days earlier he had stopped making breakfasts that neither of them wanted. Staring at the condensation on his window, at the flecks of morning rain, he marvelled at the ease with which he had been deceiving himself.

He stayed in his room for the rest of the morning. When

he realised that he wasn't going to sleep any more, he sat up and leafed through the heap of Nennius' Sunday colour supplements next to his bed. Gazing at the adverts for holidays in the Far East and versatile dresses for women, he tried to order his thoughts about what Nennius had written.

He didn't suspect for a moment that it was meant to be the truth. In a sense, that made it all the more disappointing. For Nennius had been applying himself to nothing deeply serious down there. He had only been making up a story: a beginning, a middle, and – presumably, somewhere – an end. Quinn saw it as a substitute for sexual activity, or even (and this woeful possibility numbed him) as a sexual stimulant.

Quinn also considered that Nennius had left the pages on the desk purely for him to find. But why? Why?

Early in the afternoon Quinn went down to the kitchen and made himself a sandwich. Nennius had already eaten.

Through the kitchen window Quinn saw him at the foot of the garden, poised above the upturned woman's bicycle from the shed. Quinn had always presumed that it had belonged to Nennius' wife. If so, it was the only physical indication that she had ever existed. He watched Nennius spinning its back wheel, checking its alignment, stopping it, adjusting the position of the brake-blocks, spinning it again, on and on.

Nennius looked up, saw Quinn, and raised his eyebrows. Quinn nodded to him, then took his sandwich to his room and shut himself back inside. He spent the afternoon listening to a phone-in programme on his radio. When dusk fell he changed into his tracksuit and went for a five-mile run.

He was badly out of condition. The cold air bloated his mouth and made his jaw hang down painfully as he fought for breath. And there was a strange smell on the streets. An acrid smell of decay, like escaped gas, but much more sickeningly sweet.

Nennius wasn't in the house when Quinn got back. A note on the kitchen table explained that he had been called out on a big emergency job, rewiring a pizzeria. Quinn was surprised to find the note, surprised to find that Nennius had decided to resume work. And, although he knew where the restaurant was, he had already decided to stop following Nennius. He couldn't follow a man to the end of a story. Instead, exhausted by his run, he went upstairs and fell asleep in the bath.

He woke with a start when Nennius slammed the back door on his return home. Quickly Quinn dried himself and withdrew to his room. He wasn't ready to see Nennius. Not yet. He was still too confused. But the clamour of the music told him that Nennius had gone straight down to his office.

As Quinn imagined the big man inserting a disc into the word processor, and picking up his repugnant story at the point at which he had left it, he began to quake.

He quaked throughout that night, while asleep and while awake, as phrases, words, scenes and events from the story chewed at him. In the morning he stayed in bed until he heard Nennius leave the house, trying to envisage a future for them both which could somehow grow out of this present.

There was no note this time on the kitchen table. Quinn descended to the office and consulted Nennius' work-log. He had booked in the job at the pizzeria for the next five days. The pile of pages lay on the desk, although it had been moved to the other side of the word processor. Quinn lifted all the pages save the last one. There was no new material.

He returned in a rush to the kitchen, knowing that, in the end, he would read the story again.

Still quaking, he took two bin-liners full of dirty clothes to the launderette. When he returned two hours later he cooked himself a meal, then laid and lit a log fire in the front room. He stretched out in front of it, drinking steadily from a quarter-bottle of whisky. When he realised that passers-by were looking in at him from the street, he closed the curtains. He fell asleep where he lay, the half-empty bottle at his side, and woke only when Nennius came in and touched his shoulder.

It was dark. The fire behind him had gone out. 'Are you all right?' Nennius asked softly, bending down in his overcoat.

But Quinn could think of no answer that would satisfy, so he used Nennius' arm to help him to his feet, thanked him, then walked unsteadily from the room.

He slept soundly that night but woke up midway through Saturday morning with a nagging hangover. He was aware that Nennius would be at the pizzeria all day. As he washed, shaved and breakfasted, he knew that he was going to go back to Nennius' story. It was no longer possible to stay away.

He took two small cans of beer down to the office. After an hour's rereading, he fetched another two cans from the kitchen. He continued to pore over the pages, drinking in small sips.

He was calmer than he had been in the small hours of Thursday morning. If he felt like crying, it was out of frustration, not alarm or disappointment. For now he glimpsed a familiar Nennius behind certain choices of word and in particular turns of phrase. And his frustration came from his own inability to understand *why* Nennius had chosen to place himself inside this story.

Quinn no longer saw it as unadulterated fantasy. There were too many fragments of truth in it. (Too many fragments, that was, of what Quinn knew to be the truth; and he asked himself how much more of it might be grounded in fact.) As he took the empty beer-cans up to the bin in the kitchen, he wondered whether Nennius *had*, after all, intended it to be a kind of autobiography. He saw the possibility that in some way 'the island' and 'the woman' and all the rest of it really did mean something to him. An island had, Quinn remembered, come into that crazy story he had told him on the night of the beating-up. An island and the voice of a woman.

Standing at the sink, peering into the gloom of the garden, the sweet smell of decay seemed to be rising up through the kitchen floorboards. Quinn had arrived at a large moment in his life. He was deeply frightened – for Nennius, for himself, and for any future they might still have together.

He felt sure that he had to *do* something. Already he knew what it was. It wasn't necessarily a brave thing. It could even have been seen as disloyal, as another betrayal. But Quinn knew that he had to do it – because he simply couldn't go on alone with this kind of uncertainty.

He pulled on his jacket, checked that he had enough money in his wallet, and fetched the story from the office. Hugging it to his chest, he took it directly to the copying shop four doors down from the cinema. He ran off a photocopy of the sheaf of pages, then jogged back to the house. He returned the original story to its place in the office and took the copy up to his room. While he was slipping it into his blue canvas shoulder-bag, Nennius drew up in his van beyond the back fence.

Quinn watched him coming through the gate, tossing away the stub of a cigarette, grimacing at the woman's bicycle which he had left standing outside the shed, then passing on. He looked tired. Appallingly tired.

'I can't do it alone,' Quinn said to himself, stepping back out of sight. 'I'm sorry, David. I can't get us out of this on my own.'

At ten o'clock on Sunday morning Quinn was on the road and heading north. Crossing the river, it occurred to him that Rachel might be at church. She could well have been the religious type. If she was, Quinn was prepared to wait for her return.

He knew he had to approach her apologetically. He was in no position to demand anything. And he had to avoid becoming upset. He didn't think there was any great danger of his becoming upset, but he couldn't be sure. He couldn't be sure of anything on his own. That was why he had to see Rachel. That was why he couldn't go on without her help.

He turned into her quiet tree-lined road. In the daylight it looked even more inhospitable than it had done at night. He dismounted and wheeled his Honda through the silence. Passing one driveway, he saw an old man cleaning his car. Quinn smiled, but the man looked away.

A small car stood in the drive leading to Rachel's house. Quinn parked his bike alongside it. There were two labelled bells beside the front door. Quinn pressed the lower bell, then turned his back on the house. He gazed up at the threatening sky and adjusted the shoulder-bag slung over his back. When he heard the door open, he twisted round.

'Hello?' said a blue-eyed man in running kit. There was a towel draped around his neck. He was about six feet tall and looked combative. It was the man Quinn had seen at Rachel's window in the middle of the previous week. Quinn smiled politely and offered his hand. The man took it. His handshake was firm.

'Would it be possible to speak to Rachel?' Quinn asked. The words came out in a tumble. His toes were curling inside his boots.

'Can I ask what this is about?' said the man.

'I'd just like a word with Rachel, if that's all right. I've got something for her. It won't take a minute.'

The man looked into Quinn's eyes but said nothing. His longish fair hair was matted with damp.

'I'm terribly sorry to be bothering you like this,' Quinn went on, to fill a silence which was becoming awkward.

'Well, actually,' the man said, 'Rachel is in the bath. Could I be of any help?'

'Ah,' Quinn said. 'Really I have to see Rachel.'

The man shrugged. 'In that case, you'd better come in and wait.'

He stepped back, then to one side, allowing Quinn to pass. They entered a spartan sitting-room almost side by side. There was a sofa and an armchair covered in brown needlecord. It was a draughty severe room; not at all the sort of room that Quinn had expected Rachel to have. The man showed Quinn to a straight-backed wooden chair beside a bureau.

'I could come back later,' Quinn suggested, hovering.

The man shook his head. 'There's someone here for you!' he called out to Rachel from just inside the doorway as Quinn sat down.

'Who?' Rachel yelled back.

The man glanced at Quinn and raised his eyebrows.

'My name's Quinn.'

The man repeated his name for Rachel.

Quinn smiled at his fingers, which were drumming against the crash-helmet. He started to rock back and forth.

The man wouldn't stop looking at him. He had folded his arms, and was leaning against the door-frame.

Quinn stopped rocking. The room smelt strongly of dogs, and also of coal-dust, although there was only an electric fire. A small piano stood against the wall next to the bureau. The pale green carpet needed Hoovering.

Absurd conversational ideas crowded into Quinn's head. He screwed up his face to make them go away. He knew that when Rachel eventually appeared he would have to try very hard not to become upset.

She came in with a towel wrapped around her head, and was wearing a sweatshirt and baggy trousers. The skin on her face appeared to be translucent. She looked at Quinn dubiously from behind the man's shoulder.

'Could you just give us a moment, darling?' Quinn heard her whisper.

The man pulled himself away from the door-frame and disappeared in the direction of the front door. Quinn knew that he was going to be listening out in the hall.

He stood as Rachel entered the room. 'I can understand why your friend is annoyed at being disturbed on a Sunday . . . ,' he began at once, a craven grin on his face.

Rachel indicated that he should sit again. She herself perched on the arm of the sofa.

'Matthew is my husband, Quinn,' she said, loosening the towel and rubbing at her hair. 'And, as a matter of fact, I'm a bit annoyed myself. I know you followed me home the other evening. Now this. I don't mean to sound harsh, but there are better ways of going about these things. Do you see what I mean? Oh, Christ. . . .'

Suddenly Quinn had started to cry. He couldn't make himself stop. These tears had been imminent for days, weeks. He felt almost relieved.

As he cried he tried to laugh. A sliver of spittle trailed from his mouth. Rachel kneeled before him, offering a rolled-up tissue from her pocket. Quinn took it. He saw that the tips of her long fingers were still corrugated from the bathwater. Matthew was back in the doorway. Quinn turned to him, wiping his face.

'I'm sorry, sir,' he sighed, again attempting to laugh at his own fear and guilt and shame. 'I'm so sorry about this.'

'What is it Quinn?' Rachel asked, still kneeling. 'Why have you come?'

Sniffing, Quinn pulled the bag on to his lap and unbuckled it. He took out the photocopy of Nennius' story. The top page had been folded almost in half. Quinn smoothed out the crease. Rachel motioned Matthew away.

'What's this?' she asked, standing, then coming around to Quinn's side.

'I don't know what it is,' Quinn gasped, trying to retrieve himself. 'That's why I've brought it to you. David wrote it. I found it on his desk last Wednesday night. And I made this copy. For you.'

He shrugged, swallowed, smeared the tears from his cheek, then looked up.

'I really don't understand what it is,' he went on. 'It's a kind of story, but I've never read anything like it.' He inhaled deeply and at last managed to regulate his breathing. 'Perhaps, I thought, you might be able to explain it to me. And tell me why David is writing it. I thought you might be able to tell me what I should *do*.'

Rachel frowned at the top sheet, but made no move to take it. 'You say you found it on David's desk?' she asked. 'Did he leave it out on purpose for you to read?' She paused. 'And does he know that you've brought it here?'

Quinn looked down. He had known she would have reservations. She liked to do things by the book. He hadn't expected her to approve of the way he was going about this. But he wasn't going to lie, even now.

Reaching beneath the story, he buckled up his bag again. Then, because he had nothing to lose from doing so, he took a biro from a small stone pot on the bureau and printed his address and telephone number above the first paragraph on the top sheet. As he stood, he placed the story on the chair.

'You can just throw it away if you want to,' he said, staring into Rachel's midriff. 'I know that what I've done is wrong. And I'm sorry about following you, and about everything else I've done that's wrong. But I'm doing it all because I love him, Rachel. And I just want everything to be the way it used to be between him and me.'

Quickly he left the room, almost bumping into Matthew as he turned into the hall. When he had let himself out of the house he paused. Then he ran to his bike, crouched down and pressed his forehead against the cold upholstery of the saddle. He was remembering, as if from a very long time ago, what he had just said: he had said that he loved Nennius.

He had never until that moment expressed his love for anyone. And he had meant what he had said. It had been true. Despite the vicious fight in the lavatory, despite the shock of the story, Quinn really did *love* Nennius.

Involuntarily he looked up. He felt sure he could hear laughter, high above his head.

3

Matthew closed the front door. Rachel was in the hall, the towel hanging down from her hand on to the parquet floor. She saw him shaking his head, then looked away. She guessed what he was going to say. But this time, she knew, he had a genuine case.

Matthew raised a hand to his temple. 'I'm sorry, Rachel,' he said slowly, 'but I don't like the way this is going. I'm not happy about these people following you home, coming here.'

Rachel heard Quinn start up his motorbike outside. So soon after the shock of his visit, she felt unable to say a word.

Matthew shrugged. 'I know how valuable the work is,' he persisted. 'I know that. But I think you're getting drawn in too far.' He paused. 'I mean, you went drinking with one of them. You're not supposed to do that, are you?'

Rachel smiled. 'I didn't "go drinking",' she said. 'A client just wanted to try to talk to me.'

'Yes, I know, I know. I don't doubt your motives for a moment. You just seem to have got yourself too caught up in it all.' He closed his eyes and sighed; they had covered this ground so many times before. 'But I really would prefer it if you did something less ... risky. Really, Rachel. I'm getting scared.'

Rachel looked across at him. 'You don't have to be, darling. I promise you.'

He met her eyes. 'But you don't know the first thing about these people. *Anyone* can walk into that place of yours. You're right in the firing-line. Every minute that you spend there, I'm knotted up with worry.'

Rachel turned and wandered back into the sitting-room.

She saw the photocopied script on the chair and looked away. There was too much to think about, too many considerations to make. If she were to read that script now, knowing that one client had supplied it to her without the knowledge of another, she knew that she would have to resign anyway.

Matthew followed her into the room.

'It's just going too far, Rachel,' he said. His voice quivered strangely between pique and plaintiveness. 'These people are asking too much of you. Coming to your home, making you go to the pub. . . .'

'Oh, please don't keep talking about the pub,' Rachel said. 'And I wish you wouldn't call them "these people".'

She shook her head at the script. It *was* all going too far; and so, she knew, was she.

Matthew had said that he didn't doubt her motives in lavishing attention on perfect strangers. But Rachel knew that at some level he was jealous – and that he had a right to be. She was almost readier to listen to a Quinn or a David Nennius than to keep nursing her own husband through his depression. She recognised that, and she disliked it in herself, but there didn't seem to be anything she could do about it.

And from where she stood she could easily read Quinn's address and phone number.

Her morose gaze fell to the first brief paragraph, then to the longer second. She read them, against her better judgement, standing there with the towel trailing behind her, and with Matthew just ten feet away.

'I know you're sick of me going on about this,' Matthew said, coming across to her.

'What?' Rachel looked up dizzily.

'I know you hate me nagging you. But I do think I'm right about this.'

Rachel shrugged, smiled, and looked across at the window. It hadn't yet started to rain. She wished that she was out under that grey sky, alone, just until the rain began. And she wished that she could sit down and read what David Nennius had written – whatever repercussions that might have on her own future – because in reading it perhaps she could help him.

Him, and even poor Quinn, too, either as a Samaritan or just as a private person drawn almost compulsively to strangers in despair.

She smelt the sweat on Matthew from his morning run.

'If you carry on being a Samaritan,' he said, 'I can see big trouble.'

'From whom?' asked Rachel, turning to him. 'From you or from the clients?'

He flushed, but he wouldn't be deflected. 'You can't see how embroiled you are, Rachel. You can't see yourself from the outside.'

'Like you can?' she snapped.

As soon as she said it she felt bad. She knew that Matthew only ever saw her from the outside. He watched her constantly from a position of imagined safety. It was as if he didn't dare to see, even for a moment, how *she* looked at things – or how she had begun to look at him.

'I do love you,' she said, with complete honesty, before she had time to stop herself.

Matthew raised his eyebrows. He clearly believed that she had said it to soften him up for some more wounding thrust.

'No,' she said, smiling. 'I do.'

Matthew glanced aside. 'I didn't know that was the issue.'

They stared at each other, both of them becoming aware of how deep this issue could go.

'For what it's worth,' he went on, 'I love you back – more than I want to sometimes.' Again he glanced away. 'And I know how hateful that sounds too.'

Rachel continued to smile. In the past year they had often spoken of their love for each other, sincerely enough, but rarely when they were touching. The words had their own power but they remained as words, untranslated into any more reliable kind of language.

It hadn't always been that way between them. Rachel remembered how different it had been before this prolonged adjournment in Matthew's life; and his memory was a lot better than hers. Suddenly the pity that she now felt for herself was as nothing in comparison with the sympathy which she felt for him.

Matthew came and kissed her on the mouth. She tasted the salt on his lips. It had been a fearful kiss, the kiss of a man on the outside. Rachel held him close.

'You need a bath,' she said, raising her arms and draping them around his neck.

'You need to write someone a letter,' he replied, staring down into her eyes. 'The Director of your Centre, or whoever. Please, Rachel.'

Rachel rested her head against his chest. She gazed at the manuscript on the high-backed chair beside the bureau and imagined herself reading it while Matthew was in the bathroom. Its first two paragraphs had lodged almost word-for-word in her head. She wanted to read it more urgently than, in the present circumstances, she wished to remain a Samaritan.

'I'll resign,' she whispered, so softly that Matthew had to ask her to say it again.

'And you'll send that script back?' he said after they had kissed.

'Yes,' she told him.

4

From Sunday until Wednesday, Quinn didn't leave the house. He thought it less and less likely that Rachel would get in touch. To take the edge off his anxiety he kept himself busy. He prepared a number of meals for freezing and gave the house a thorough clean. He even painted over a damp patch on the front-room wall. Once he went into the office, to find that the story had gone from its place on the desk.

Nennius came home late each evening from the pizzeria. He would spend several hours in the office before going up to bed. Although Quinn saw him rarely, he felt as if he were never out of the big man's shadow.

Then, at six o'clock on Wednesday morning, Nennius shook him awake and handed him a mug of tea. 'I could use you today,' he said. 'I have to have this whole job wrapped up by nine tonight. I could use some help in making good the plaster – if you're interested.'

He left the room. Half an hour later, as the van backed out into the flooded alley, Quinn was sitting up alongside him.

Quinn knew that by going out with Nennius for the day he was admitting that, once again, he was on his own. It seemed implausible that Rachel should have read the story and then failed to make contact with him. He could only presume that she hadn't felt able to read it, that her sense of propriety – or possibly her husband's – had been too much for her.

Quinn stared out of the side-window at the gutters running with filthy water. He felt deflated. Alone he had to salvage his relationship with the man whom he loved. And, in a way, this daunting certainty seemed almost preferable to floating in the limbo of the past few days as he had awaited Rachel's decision.

They collected some sacks of plaster *en route*. Quinn loaded them into the back of the van while Nennius paid. He wondered how much more of the story Nennius might have written in the previous week. When they resumed their journey, he longed to ask Nennius what happened next, after he had met 'the black girl'. But he wasn't ready to tell the story's author that he had read it. This wasn't the time or the place. But perhaps, he told himself, he could do so that evening, when they got back to the house.

The rest of that day with Nennius was strangely satisfactory. For several hours they were in separate parts of the large restaurant, so there was no sense of communion through their work. Quinn found the work itself to his liking. It made a change from his usual daily business, and was a welcome distraction from all his anxieties.

Both Nennius and the proprietor complimented him on the neatness of his plastering. Towards the end of the day he remembered, with surprise, some of the *good* moments he'd had as a conventional wage-earner, back in the life that he usually preferred to forget.

The job was finished by seven-thirty. The delighted proprietor paid Nennius on the spot. He paid in cash, generously rounding up the final figure from nineteen hundred to two thousand pounds. The three of them then sat round a small table drinking beer for an hour. The proprietor told some lengthy jokes, during the course of which Quinn watched Nennius' face closely.

He hadn't shaved all week. His eyes looked glazed. But there was a softness about his expression which had recently been missing. If he didn't look happy, then at least he didn't look hunted. He didn't seem to be *struggling* any more. It gave Quinn the confidence he needed to go ahead and force a confrontation later that evening.

Nennius tossed him the keys to the van before they sprinted out through the rain. For a ghastly moment, Quinn thought he wanted to be driven again to the roadside lavatory.

'Home?' he asked as he started the engine.

'Home,' Nennius replied, nodding as he opened a packet of cigarettes.

The route home took them past the Samaritans Centre.

Quinn barely saw it through the driving rain. He guessed that Rachel would be in there, doing the right thing for someone else. And he regretted having shown her the story. For what, after all, could she have told him about Nennius? What could she have explained that he didn't already know?

Quinn saw that Nennius himself avoided looking at the Centre. Instead, he was pulling the wad of notes from his coat pocket. He counted the money again, then separated out five twenties.

'Here,' he said, folding them once and pressing them against Quinn's thigh. 'Thanks for your help.'

Quinn reached down for the money. When he saw how much it was, he tried to give it back.

Nennius had already turned his head away, to stare at the floodlit façade of the old Infirmary. 'Easy come, easy go,' he said with a shrug. Then he pointed. 'Pull over at that chip shop. You don't want to have to start cooking when we get back.'

Nennius fetched two fish suppers, which they ate in the van while listening to the radio. 'David,' Quinn said quietly after he had rolled up Nennius' paper with his own and dumped it in a bin on the pavement, 'do you think we could talk when we get home?'

'All right,' Nennius replied after a moment's pause. 'If that's what you really want.' He turned to Quinn and smiled.

Neither of them said a word during the last stretch of the journey. Quinn was thinking ahead. He could see them seated opposite each other at the kitchen table, a bottle of whisky between them, perhaps some music playing through the extension speakers. He saw himself swallowing, then confessing that he had read Nennius' story. And then he saw Nennius lighting up a cigarette, smiling in a chastened but forgiving way, then beginning to put it all back together again. . . .

Apprehensive but hopeful, he slowed to a crawl before entering the alley at the back of the house. There was scarcely enough room for such a wide van. Several parked bicycles narrowed the passage even further. From thirty yards Quinn saw two blobs of red light in Nennius' parking-space. Nennius noticed them, too, and sat forward to peer through the windscreen.

They drew closer. Quinn made out a long car, the colour of mud, parked askew to the rear of their garden. The overhead light was on inside the car. A figure, possibly reading, was hunched in the driver's seat.

Quinn pulled up behind. 'I'll ask him to move, shall I?' he said to Nennius, who was leaning almost across him to get a closer look at the car and its driver.

'Yes,' he replied, still looking hard. 'Leave the keys in the ignition. I'll park it.'

Quinn heard Nennius sliding across into the driver's seat as he climbed out, planting first one foot into an unavoidable puddle and then, swearing, the other. It was while he was casting about for a drier foothold that the evening fell apart.

The figure in the car, having seen Quinn emerging, stepped out into the rain. A tall man in a red rally-jacket, he put up an umbrella and called out a greeting which Quinn didn't hear. He couldn't hear because of the roar of the van. Nennius had ground it into reverse gear, drawn back a little way, then careered forward to the end of the alley and out into the road beyond.

'Bugger him!' said the man, coming close enough to Quinn to hold his umbrella over them both.

Quinn stared into the man's face. He looked a dozen or so years older than Nennius, dark-eyed, alert, and with a very short haircut which made his ears stand out. 'I wrote to him, you see,' the man went on. 'Told him I was coming. I drove three hundred miles to get here and I've been waiting in that car since half-past five. It's not very funny.'

They both looked up the alley, into the emptiness where Nennius' van had been. Quinn could smell alcohol on the man's breath. He had never seen him before and didn't know what to say. In the event the man solved the problem by passing the umbrella into his left hand and offering his right.

'I'm Meredith,' he said as they shook. 'William Meredith. Would you be Quinn?'

The Christian name ricocheted around inside Quinn's head. *'William?'* he said almost in alarm, drawing his hand away.

'That's right,' the man laughed and cocked his head. 'David's given you all the dirt on me, then, has he?'

'What is it you want?' Quinn asked in little more than a whisper.

'I just want to talk to David,' he said, still very close. 'It's all above board.'

Quinn had backed off into the rain, his mouth slightly open. The man called William looked up the alley, then passed the umbrella back into his right hand. 'Don't get so bothered,' he said. 'I told you: it's all above board. I don't mean him any harm. He's got hold of the wrong end of the stick, that's all. Look, perhaps you and I ought to have a chat.'

Quinn frowned, and backed away further, until he was crouching beneath the eave of the garden shed on the other side of the fence. With both cold hands he drew together the lapels of his jacket. His hair was soaked through. He had to blink constantly to keep the man in focus. *William*, was all that Quinn could think. *William, William.*

'Couldn't I just come in for a cup of tea?' said Meredith.

There was something playful about the way he spoke. Something that might or might not have been patronising. 'What do you want?' Quinn asked again. 'Why won't you leave us alone?'

'Us?' Meredith raised his eyebrows. 'I don't know you from Adam, Quinn. I've got no axe to grind against you.' His face kept moving suddenly from one expression to another, and when he wasn't smiling he could look quite haggard. 'I've got no axe to grind against David, either, if only he'd ease up for a minute. It's nothing to do with me and him, you see. I'm only the go-between here.'

He hesitated, looked penetratingly at Quinn, then continued: 'It's about Art, as a matter of fact. His son. I just want to talk to David about his son. You knew he had one of those, didn't you?'

Quinn nodded. Nennius had never mentioned his son by name. Quinn had never seen a photo of him, and there was no evidence that he had ever lived in the house. But Quinn knew that there was a son, just as there had once been a wife.

'Look,' said Meredith, 'are we going to go in, or what? It's bloody stupid standing around out here.'

'David's son,' Quinn said in a hesitant voice, doggedly holding his ground. 'Is he all right?'

Meredith looked away. 'Yes, yes. He's all right. There's nothing to worry about on that score.' He stared thoughtfully at the cowering figure under the eave. 'Look, Quinn, you're a pal of David's by the sound of it. Can't you try to persuade him to have a word with me? You could be there as well, if that'd make things any easier. It's like I told you: there's nothing to worry about.' Momentarily he squinted. 'For him or for you.'

Quinn had plenty to worry about. The word *William* was still pulsing in his head. There was absolutely nothing he could do with it. The name became more insistent. Quinn closed his eyes. The rain seemed louder in the dark. He could hear the occasional whining of cars up in the street in front of the house. He kept his eyes closed for some time. When he opened them, Meredith was holding the umbrella between his upper arm and his side and was scribbling something on a piece of card.

'Here,' he said, holding out the card to Quinn when he had finished. 'That's where you can reach me. Give me a call when David wants to talk. Any time, day or night, at work or at home. I can only do so much on my own.'

Quinn took the card. Printed on it were the words *W. R. Meredith Transport. Road Haulage Contractors. Commercial Vehicle Repairs. Recovery Breakdown Service*, with a Lancashire address and telephone number. Scrawled above it was a further telephone number, against which he had printed *ANY TIME!* and underlined it three times.

Quinn put it in his jacket pocket and said nothing. He could only wait as Meredith turned and walked to his car. Quickly he let down the umbrella and threw it into the back.

'It's really not funny, this,' he shouted, his hand clutching the door. 'I mean, I've been out here for bloody hours and that's my own house there.'

He turned now to face Quinn, his eyebrows raised. The rain was drumming against his head. 'I don't suppose you knew that, did you? That you're living in my house?' He grinned. 'Ah, well. Why should you?'

Quinn watched in silence as he climbed into his car, started the engine, backed up, raised his hand stiffly, then inched along to the end of the alley.

Quinn remained outside for a further ten minutes. Then, when he was so wet that the rain seemed to be coursing right through him, he went indoors.

5

When Nennius stopped driving he found himself in the cul-de-sac beside the Samaritans Centre. He stayed behind the wheel, breathing deeply, half-listening to a play on the radio, pressing back the memory of the man he had seen in the alley. Then, as the rain eased, he walked down to the pub he had visited with Rachel.

Standing straight-backed at the saloon bar he drank four neat whiskies and gradually recovered his steadiness. His fifth was bought by a man who came in from the pool room, a stocky schoolteacher in his early thirties. Years before, he and Nennius had played cricket for the same local club.

'Are you getting enough work, David?' the teacher asked.

'More than I can handle,' Nennius replied.

'I can believe that,' he laughed. 'You look shagged out!' He winked. 'You should come up to the club. We could have a beer. We might even get you playing again.' Nennius smiled, drank up, and headed for the door.

The rain had stopped. Nennius walked slowly back to the van. He climbed in and switched on the engine. *'Now!'* he pleaded. 'Why can't it be *now*?' But he knew she was waiting until he had disgorged the entire story.

He took in two lungfuls of air.

Then, as he exhaled, he reared up and punched the cab roof so hard that blood showed immediately at the back of his yellow mitten.

He gasped when the pain shot through his arm, and punched the roof again. He kept on punching it, using both

106

fists, disfiguring the metal, until he collapsed heavily into the windscreen and steering-wheel.

When he regained consciousness, he felt a dull ache in his cheek. His hands were screaming. Both mittens were bloodied, but the left hand hurt more. He tried to flex his fingers. To his surprise, they all moved.

He glanced up and saw an old woman in a headscarf at the neck of the cul-de-sac. She was watching him uncertainly. A dog sat on the wet pavement beside her. Keeping his left hand flat, Nennius found first gear and moved forward. When he swung round into the road the woman led the dog away.

There had been an accident at the first main junction. Behind the police cordon, Nennius made out two twisted cars. An officer on duty saluted him familiarly and directed him to follow the diverted traffic. The police knew his van. They were used to seeing him out on call at all hours. Nennius drove slowly, using the palms of both hands. By this route, it would take him about fifteen minutes to get to Melissa's house.

He parked at the near end of her street. A fresh wind squalled around him. He buttoned up his overcoat as he walked along under the street-lamps. The throbbing at his cheek and in his hands prevented him from thinking in any kind of sequence about the woman, or the end before the end, or the man he had seen in the alley.

There were no lights in Melissa's windows. Nennius walked backwards across the street, looking up to see if there was a glow of light coming from the bathroom. There was nothing. Faintly in the distance he heard music, mixed in with the hum of the wind, and perhaps some laughter. He stepped up to Melissa's front door and rang the bell.

No one answered. He rang a second time and a third. Then he began to shout.

What he shouted made little sense. Loud though his voice was, he wasn't articulating words or thoughts. He was making the noise of a man who had done and seen and heard enough. For a moment he fell silent, and again he thought he could hear music and voices, but closer now. He threw back his head, closed his eyes, and yelled at the sky. A continuous billowing moan. When his breath ran out, he heard a man's voice addressing him from behind.

Nennius turned and saw people staring at him from their doorways. He saw faces at some of the lighted upstairs windows. And directly in front of him he saw a man of about his own age, reaching out and indicating that he should move along the street. 'The person who lives here is around the corner,' he explained. 'At my place.'

The man was small, with a greying moustache and a boyish smile. He wore a short car-coat and shoes with untied laces. His legs and the visible part of his chest were bare. He noticed the blood on Nennius' mittens and took his elbow. 'Come to the house,' he said. 'We'll get you sorted out. We're having a bit of a party.'

Giddy now, Nennius allowed himself to be guided along to the corner. With his head aloft, he looked to left and right, and he saw nothing. Not the silent figures in the doorways, not the faces at the windows, not the pacifying gestures which this man was making at them all. 'We'll get you sorted out,' he said over and over, as if it were a line from a song.

The sound of the party broke against them as they turned into the narrower street. A handful of men were talking in a doorway. They all wore bathing costumes. One had goggles and a snorkel. 'We're having a beachwear party,' said the man at Nennius' elbow. 'Just to keep our peckers up, you know?'

He disappeared as soon as they entered the house. It was stiflingly hot. The small shabby rooms brimmed with guests. Nennius gazed down the hall, above the heads, into the kitchen, where people cavorted in a sandpit. The music was deafening. A deeply tanned girl in a red bikini turned away from a conversation and raised her arms to Nennius' shoulders.

He inclined his head. She kissed him on the lips, giggled, and shrank back into the press. Nennius stood still, a fierce neuralgic pain swarming through the right side of his face. Then he took off his coat, and threw it on to a heap of clothing just inside the front room.

An older woman, in a modest blue one-piece costume, took his arm. She shouted that he was to follow her upstairs to the

108

bathroom. Nennius did as he was told. She nodded towards the edge of the bath, on which he sat, then she set to work on his hands: peeling off his mittens, cleaning and treating the cuts, covering them with plasters snipped from a single strip.

Neither spoke until she had finished. Her perfume and the confined space and the buzz of the striplight were making Nennius' head reel. 'Thank you,' he said to her, standing. 'You've been very kind.'

'Go down and join in,' she said, loading the first-aid materials back into the cabinet. 'Get yourself a drink. You look as if you could do with one.'

Dutifully Nennius found his way down to the kitchen. He stood by the sink, lit a cigarette and accepted a paper cup of frothy punch. No one seemed able to keep still, even the talkers who were standing in tight clusters around the sandpit. They were all so far inside the screaming music that the entire event seemed to have been choreographed.

Most of the guests were younger than the host or the woman who had attended to Nennius' hands. The sight of so many girls in so few clothes disturbed him. He knew it was unwise to stay, an unnecessary risk. But he didn't go. He kept on drinking, trying to forget what he had seen in the alley behind his house, watching the girls, hoping against hope that the lips and the fetor might allow him one last release.

When the punch ran out, Nennius took a bottle of port from the draining-board and drank straight from its neck. He hadn't stopped drinking since finishing work. He recalled, then quickly forgot, that he had the best part of two thousand pounds in the pocket of his coat. He took another pull at the port and tapped his foot to the next song. The girl who had kissed him in the hall was crossing the sandpit towards the downstairs bathroom.

She was thin but not painfully so. The length of her legs both saddened and agitated Nennius. She passed so close that he saw the beads of perspiration at her collarbone, above which she wore a fine gold chain. She smiled collusively up at him. 'Come in with me,' she said.

Nennius smiled, in such a way that his sadness and his agitation were equally obvious. Then he put the neck of the port-bottle back to his lips, and the girl shut herself inside the bathroom. Someone grabbed his arm: a glassy-eyed young man wearing a deck-chair like a sandwich-board. 'I hear you want to speak to me,' he said, and when Nennius frowned he went on: 'You were bashing on my front door and yelling. Or so I've been told.'

Nennius thought carefully before answering. 'I made a mistake,' he said. 'I'm sorry. I made a mistake.'

The youth reeled away, tripping and falling into the beer-streaked sand. Nennius helped him up. Then the girl in the red bikini was in front of him again, hands on hips. 'Well, we could dance,' she said. 'Couldn't we?'

She had tangled blonde shoulder-length hair, dark eyes in an oval face. There was something about the frankness of her look which reminded Nennius of the girl Rachel. No, he thought without conviction, I can't do any of the things you want me to do. I can't.

He turned and placed the port-bottle back on the draining-board. 'I really have to be going,' he told her. He went to the bathroom and remained there for ten minutes. Then it took him some time to force his way through to the front door. There was no sign of the man who had invited him. In the front room two of the older women had removed their bikini tops and were performing a kind of belly dance. The front door was open. Nennius was on the pavement when he heard her call out. He turned.

'You've forgotten something,' said the girl in the red bikini. She was standing on the doorstep, pulling on Nennius' huge overcoat. In her left hand was a bulging shoulder-bag; in her right a pair of red high-heeled shoes. She stooped to slip on the shoes. 'OK,' she said, pulling the lapels together at her neck, settling her bag over her shoulder and holding up the hem of the coat as if it were a ball-gown, 'I'm ready.'

At first Nennius said nothing. Looking at her, he put a cigarette in his mouth and lit it. She came towards him. Throwing down the spent match, he told her: 'I think it would be better if you stayed here.'

'Where are you parked?' she said, passing him. 'I only want a lift home.'

'Where do you live?'

'We can discuss that when we find the car,' she said over her shoulder.

'I'm serious,' Nennius said, following her up to Melissa's street. 'Please go back inside.' He cleared his throat. 'I'm no use to you.'

'Which way now?' she asked at the junction.

Nennius stood drawing on his cigarette. The girl pursed her lips. He wanted very badly to kiss her. From the moment that she had invited him into the bathroom he had been nursing an erection. He closed his eyes and saw brightness. When he opened them there was shadow – the shadow of the only woman. 'Go back to the party,' he said unevenly. 'This isn't a good idea.'

'Well, I'm heading *this* way,' she said, pointing in the correct direction. Then she broke into a trot, skipped, and swung herself easily around the first street-lamp. She rushed past Melissa's house, past the windows and doorways from which Nennius had earlier been observed. Nennius followed, striding deeper into the woman's shadow.

When the girl reached his van, he shouted for her to stop. He nodded as she turned, threw away his cigarette, climbed up into the cab and opened the passenger-door for her. He was shuddering, but not from the cold. They embraced and kissed on the long front seat before he started the engine. She was wearing a pleasant scent, like the smell of children's sweets. And beneath the perfume and the taste of her lip-gloss were the livelier smells of clean skin and perspiration.

Nennius' stomach began to tighten. For the other odour was there, too – not on the girl, not on him, either, but coming from the fact of what they were doing there, the sheer impossibility of it. 'My flat's only ten minutes away,' the girl said quietly, the gaiety gone from her voice. 'The girls I share with are still at the party. We'll have the place to ourselves.'

Nennius drew away, shaking his head. 'Please,' was all he could say. But he couldn't take his hand from the smoothness of her thigh inside his coat. She pressed herself against him. He turned to her and they kissed again. Her mouth was warm. The kiss lasted until he began to fight for breath.

'You're beautiful,' he gasped. 'But you've got to go.'

She slid her mouth away from his, across his cheek, and put her lips to his ear. 'We don't have to be doing this here,' she whispered.

Coughing, he pulled away again, and raised his hand to his mouth. He was starting to retch. The vomit had coursed up as far as his throat. He pawed at the inside of his door but couldn't locate the handle to wind down the window. At last he succeeded, then hung his head over the side to take in great mouthfuls of the damp night air.

The beautiful girl hauled herself up close behind him. Nennius pushed her back with his elbow. The fetor had filled the van and flooded the whole of the inside of him. Filthy, ammoniac, lavatorial. The stench of death in a dark place. He was breathing it in, breathing it out. There was nothing but the stench: the stench sent by *her*. For ten years she had been sending it, the only gift he had ever received from that most vindictive of all women; the stench with which she had forced him to forgo all women save herself.

Then he felt the shifting beneath him, saw the gore-stained lips parting: a face he could never forget, from the end before the end, twisting now into the loveliest smile, male and female, living and waiting.

'It'll pass,' the girl was saying. 'I felt bad myself around midnight. I think it was the punch. . . .'

Nennius screwed himself up. '*Get out of the van,*' he was able to shout before gagging. '*Keep the coat. But go. Just go.*'

He hunched himself again over the side of the van and closed his eyes. He could hear movement behind him. Her fingers were at his elbow. 'I'm sorry,' she murmured. 'I didn't think you meant it.' He felt the touch of her lips on the back of his head – nothing more than a kiss goodbye.

Then the stench seemed to burst within itself, flooding Nennius with his own unassuageable guilt. '*No!*' he choked, flinging back his arm. '*No! No!*'

At last he heard the sound of her door opening and softly closing. He heard the click of her heels on the pavement. And when that click had receded a little way he dared to lift his head and watch her. She was moving quickly but not hurrying, the bag slung over her tanned shoulder, her blonde hair tapering into her virtually bare back. She wore nothing but the bikini. In the thickening darkness before dawn, she looked magnificent.

Nennius slumped sideways on to the seat, reprieved from nothing but himself.

His coat was there, neatly folded, the wad of cash bulking out the pocket. Still panting, using the coat as a pillow, he drifted into a sleep that was beyond the reach of loving.

An hour later the passenger-door opened. Nennius woke at once, and looked up to see Quinn.

6

Quinn drove Nennius home in silence. Snow was falling again. Large flakes seemed to be swirling up at them from the surface of the road. He had been out searching the main roads for over an hour. Then he had remembered the narrow street near the allotments in which Nennius had twice pulled over during the midnight drives.

Nennius had helped Quinn to load his bike into the back of the van. He'd been willing to go along with whatever the younger man suggested. Now Quinn kept his eyes on the road and off the blood-smeared dents in the cab roof and the plasters on Nennius' hands. There would be time to talk when they got home. Time enough.

In the kitchen, as Quinn was flushing water into the kettle for tea, Nennius spoke first. 'I have to be off at seven-thirty,' he said. 'Estimating. I'll go and get some proper sleep.'

Quinn switched on the kettle and turned slowly. He couldn't leave it there.

'We'll talk this evening,' Nennius said from the doorway when he saw the dissatisfaction on Quinn's face. 'I promise.'

Quinn held his gaze. 'I read those pages of yours,' he said, putting his hands behind his back. 'That story you're writing, I read it last week.'

Nennius looked aside. Then, to Quinn's surprise, he squatted down on his haunches and rested his forearms along his thighs. It was like the reflex action of some helpless wild animal.

'Did you want me to read it, David?' Quinn said levelly. 'Did you leave those pages out on purpose for me to read?'

Nennius glanced up, just for a moment, and Quinn saw

terror in his face. The kettle boiled, and he turned with relief to fill the pot. He heard the floorboards creak as Nennius stood. 'Have you finished it, David,' Quinn asked over his shoulder, 'your story?'

Nennius didn't answer.

'What are you intending to do with it?' he said. 'Try to get it into a magazine or something?' He looked back as he reached for the tea-cosy. Nennius had gone.

'David!' he shouted, running out to the foot of the stairs. Nennius stared down at him from the landing.

'We'll talk this evening,' he promised again. 'This won't go on, Quinn. It can't go on.'

'Do you mean that things are going to get better?'

Nennius made no answer. Quinn narrowed his eyes; a verbal answer was as unnecessary as a candle in heaven. Immediately he decided to take a different line.

'That man in the alley last night,' he called up the stairs. 'Meredith. He didn't seem so terrible. Why did you drive away like that, David? He didn't mean you any harm. He told me he didn't mean you any harm.'

Nennius grasped the banister rail. 'You can cause harm without intending to,' he said.

Quinn took three steps up the stairs and also grabbed the banister. He had an odd notion that the banister was like a Bible, that while they both were touching it they could tell each other no lies. 'Was he the same William, David?' he asked. 'Was he the William in your story?'

Nennius turned away and entered his bedroom. Quinn climbed the stairs after him. He arrived in Nennius' room prepared to shout and even to fight.

'You can't keep running away, David,' he said in a low voice, looking not at Nennius, who was undressing on the far side of his bed, but at the naked fair-haired man on the postcard, staring out so blithely past them both. 'I think you should speak to Meredith. Why won't you see him? Why?' He glanced at Nennius' plastered hands. 'And why do you keep *hurting* yourself?'

Nennius, in only his underpants, shook his head. Then he drew back the duvet and climbed into bed.

'Talk to me, David,' Quinn said, his eyes again on the postcard. 'Please say something to me. I only want to help you.' He blinked because tears were forming. But Nennius said nothing, and the fair-haired man on the postcard seemed to be saying, *Pack it in. Leave it. What good is this doing anyone?*

Quinn looked up at the ceiling. His eyes widened. And then he roared: '*I just want to know what's happening!*'

Nennius did not flinch. Quinn recovered himself almost immediately. Panting hard, he continued in a kind of delirium: 'I'm finding this so difficult, David. For weeks, so difficult. It's been so strange. That fight you were in, that story you wrote, then the business with Meredith, and now these plasters on your hands and the blood in the cab. . . . What's been *happening*? Let me know, David. I do need to know.'

'You don't need to know,' Nennius countered, his face half-buried in his pillow. 'I regret that you know as much as you do.'

Quinn looked down at the back of him, at the exposed section of shoulder and the tangle of his hair. He thought he could hear the laughter again, even before he said it.

'But I love you, David.'

And then there was only silence, the tick of Nennius' alarm-clock, the whirring of the fridge down in the kitchen. Quinn felt as if he were floating. 'I love you in a good way,' he elaborated.

Nennius hadn't turned, but his eyes were open. A large lorry lumbered up the street and passed the house. 'I know that,' Nennius said.

Quinn flung himself down on to the bed.

He wasn't crying. His face was lost in Nennius' hair. His left hand was clawing at Nennius' solid shoulder. His knees were pressed hard, through the duvet, against Nennius' back. He wasn't crying, but his throat felt hoarse, his eyes felt tiny. It was as if he had been crying his heart out all winter.

But he was past crying now. All he could do was hold on to the little he still had. For now he felt sure that soon he would lose it all.

* * *

Nennius had no idea how long Quinn lay holding him. But, however long it lasted, the experience was extraordinary.

As soon as Quinn touched him, the voice sounded in his head. Her voice, her words, the only words. *I know you, I have found you. . . .* Endlessly she repeated them, whispering them at first, the pitch of her voice rising with each delivery, her pronunciation becoming more and more blurred, until at last there was nothing in his head but a distant banshee wail.

And Nennius was drawing comfort, even a kind of joy, from the nearness of another body. A wrong body, but human all the same, warm and concerned and alive. His excitement wasn't sexual. He wasn't aroused in the way that the girl at the party had aroused him. But Quinn's being there, close and quiet, was uncovering a light within Nennius which he thought had guttered and died years before.

Only when he could take no more of the banshee wail did Nennius slowly turn on to his back, then lever himself up on to his elbows. Quinn was loath to loosen his grip. His fingernails dug into Nennius' shoulder, but the older man was far too strong for him. Gently he took Quinn's wrists and set them away from him.

Quinn was staring, bulbous-eyed, at the ceiling. He was trembling. There was spittle at the corner of his mouth. Nennius wiped it away with a finger. Then he left the bed, walked around to Quinn's side, and helped him to his feet. With one hand under Quinn's armpit, the other pressed flat against his stomach, he led him through to his own room.

The five twenty-pound notes from the night before were lying, screwed up into balls, on the floor. Quinn allowed himself to be laid out on the bed. Carefully Nennius peeled off his jacket, his pullover, his jeans, socks and boots, and the elastic band which held his hair in place.

His slim body was still trembling in short spasms, his eyes wide open. Nennius lifted him with a single huge hand in the small of his back, drew back the duvet, and settled him beneath it. Then he sat down on the edge of the bed, and stared at his own hands. The curtains hadn't been closed. Snow was spinning fast against the window. Suddenly Quinn spoke. It was as if his voice had come in from outside the room.

'That man Meredith,' he said. 'He told me that this was his house.'

Nennius took a breath, which he held, then let go with a small sigh. He couldn't *say* it. It wasn't in him to explain any of it – beginning, middle or end. The explanations all belonged elsewhere.

He looked down into Quinn's face, at his dark hair fanned out on the pillow, and he remembered the strange lost pleasure of their embrace. There was a smile at Quinn's mouth now, nervous and abstracted.

'There's nothing you can do for me, Quinn,' Nennius said. 'I'm sorry. But I can't let you think any differently.'

Then he watched the young man turn over, still smiling, and pull the duvet over his head.

7

Rachel was reading Nennius' script for the third time when Matthew discovered that she hadn't sent it back.

She read it first on the Sunday of Quinn's visit, after writing to the Director of the Centre. *This has to be in haste,* her letter said. *For personal reasons I am resigning from the Samaritans, and my decision must take effect immediately. I'm extremely sorry to be letting you down. . . .* When Matthew took Davis for his evening walk, she fetched the script from the chair on which Quinn had left it. She read it in less than twenty minutes. Flushed and breathless, she then slipped it into her briefcase.

She took the astonishing story to work with her next morning, but only on Tuesday did she have time to read it more closely. She took it back home the next evening and hid it at the top of the airing-cupboard. In the small hours of Thursday morning she tiptoed along to the bathroom. Minutes after she'd started to read it again, perched on the edge of the bath, Matthew came and found her.

'Oh hell,' he said from the doorway, immediately recognising what she was reading. He scratched his head and repeated the one word: 'Hell, *hell.*'

Rachel looked up at him, her lips pressed together, her eyes pale with tears. She shuffled the pages together in her lap, then held the story to her chest. 'I'm just reading it, Matthew,' she said. 'I'm not doing anything else. Just reading it.'

'But *why*, Rachel?' he pleaded. 'There's nothing you can do about it now, is there?' He rubbed his hair, then his temple. 'Or didn't you resign, either?'

'I did resign,' Rachel assured him. 'But I can't switch it all off. These are real people, Matthew.' She paused and looked down at her bare feet.

Matthew leaned against the door-frame. In the study Davis was stirring, awakened by the voices. 'You look so upset,' Matthew said more softly. 'What's upsetting you?'

'This,' Rachel said, nodding at the story and clutching it more protectively.

Matthew swallowed, blinked up at the light, and pressed his fingers together. He had been working at his typewriter until only a couple of hours before, drinking beer, swaying in his chair to the rhythms of his music. Rachel realised that he was far from sober. This wasn't necessarily a problem. Drunk, he could sometimes approximate to the old easy-going Matthew.

'You can tell me about it,' he said, nodding at the story. 'You're not bound by ethics any more. Tell me – what's that stuff about?'

Rachel continued to stare at her feet, which she had set neatly side by side. She was not prepared to succumb, again, to Matthew's emotional censure. To her this was no longer a purely ethical matter. A good deal more was at stake, and not just for David Nennius and Quinn. This involved her, too – and even, by extension, her husband, with his fearful blanket refusal to come in from the outside.

'Go back to bed, darling,' she implored him. 'I'm just asking you to let me handle this in my own way.'

Matthew wouldn't go.

He came forward and sat beside her on the edge of the bath. Rachel closed her eyes as he put his arm around her shoulders. She smelt the beer on his breath. *Don't*, was what she couldn't say. Don't, don't, don't. He kissed the crown of her head. Only the formality of their love for each other stopped Rachel from pushing him away.

'Tell me,' he whispered. 'Why are you crying?'

'I was crying', Rachel replied, stiff within his embrace, 'out of helplessness.'

'But *why* exactly?' he insisted, kissing her again on that meaningless part of her head. Rachel felt far beyond the range of his language. And although she knew that her secrecy must be hurting him – her secrecy and her stubborn commitment to the outside world – she felt nothing but annoyance at his intrusion.

'Go back to bed,' she said, and kissed him on the mouth. 'Please, Matthew. Please.'

And he went, tight-lipped, without looking back. But moments later he was back in the doorway. Rachel looked up in surprise.

'I wouldn't mind so much,' he said with a caustic smile, 'if you showed a bit more interest in what *I'm* writing.'

'Oh, Matthew,' Rachel gasped. 'That's not fair. That's so unfair. I *am* interested. But you never seem to want to talk about it.'

He stopped smiling. 'That doesn't mean I want you to stop asking.'

They stared at each other. Matthew's eyes were moist now. Rachel looked away.

'I'd talk if you were genuinely interested,' he went on. 'I'd like to talk. But you're not genuinely interested, Rachel.' He raised a hand to override any interruption. 'I can't show you my work, because you're embarrassed about me trying to write. You have been from the start.'

Rachel stood. 'I'm not embarrassed, Matthew,' she lied. 'I am genuinely interested, I am. . . .'

But she could think of nothing more to say, nothing that was likely to make any difference in these circumstances.

'I'll leave you to it, then,' he said at last, turning, then retreating into their bedroom and closing the door.

Rachel sat again on the edge of the bath, still irritated, but otherwise strangely untouched by what had been said. After staring at the closed bedroom door for several minutes, she resumed her reading.

On the following morning she took David Nennius' story back to her office. She also took a list of telephone numbers for all the Samaritans who were based at the Centre.

At the end of the day, when the floor on which her firm conducted its business was virtually empty, Rachel picked up the phone. She dialled the first of three numbers which she thought might lead her to Grace. The old woman herself was no longer on the list, but her husband was. Rachel had an idea that their surname was either Pierce or Pearson, of whom there were two on the list. The second Pearson turned out to be the right one.

Grace answered, and went immediately on to the defensive. 'I've been feeling so bad about ringing you,' she said. 'It wasn't the right thing to have done at all, not from anybody's point of view—'

'Grace, listen,' Rachel interrupted. 'Can I come and see you?'

There was no reply.

'Please,' said Rachel, putting her free hand to her forehead. 'This is nothing to do with the Samaritans now. I resigned at the weekend. But I'm still concerned about David Nennius. I'm convinced that he's intending to kill himself.' She paused. 'And I've been reading something he's written.'

'What sort of thing?' Grace asked slowly. 'You mean he wrote to you?'

'This is what I want to come and talk to you about. He's written a kind of story, or possibly a part of a story, about himself. But it's a hopeless tangle of fact – or what I take to be fact – and fantasy. In places I just can't tell the two apart.' She closed her eyes. 'I was wondering if you'd be willing to help me disentangle it.'

When she fell silent she realised how loud and fast she had been talking. A phone rang in an outer office. One of Rachel's colleagues passed her doorway to take the call. He smiled at Rachel, who asked him politely if he would close her door.

'You say you've resigned—' Grace began.

'It wasn't over David Nennius,' Rachel said at once, before realising that Grace mightn't have been suggesting that it was.

'No,' she went on, 'but if you have resigned, Rachel, you really should try to let it go now.'

Yes, I know, thought Rachel. Yes, I know. Yes, I know.

'I don't think', Grace continued in a firmer, more compassionate voice, 'it would be sensible for us to meet. Not over this anyway. You should tell the Director everything you feel she needs to know, and then leave it.' She paused. 'I understand how you can get drawn in, though, Rachel. I do sympathise.'

Rachel was doodling fiercely on her notepad.

'I'm sorry about this,' Grace said into the silence. 'I feel I've put my foot in it. And I dearly hope that my call didn't have anything to do with your resignation.'

'It had nothing whatever to do with it,' Rachel told her, deciding that she had to cut corners. 'Grace,' she said almost brightly, 'you said that David Nennius was dangerous, that he could do the most awful damage. Tell me, Grace, did he do something to Melissa?'

Of course Grace didn't answer. Rachel didn't expect an answer. She had simply wanted to weigh Grace's silence.

'You see,' Rachel went on quickly, her eyes closed tight, 'I know he feels dreadfully guilty about something. He really believes that he has to die, to atone for whatever it is that he's done. And this story of his . . . well, to me it reads rather like the beginning of a very long suicide-note. So I'm just taking a shot in the dark here, but from what he's told me, and from what he's written, and from what you've told me, too, I have a strong suspicion that he did something to his wife.'

'No,' Grace said tremulously as soon as Rachel had finished. 'No, that wasn't what I was trying to tell you in my own stupid way. Please can we stop this now? There's really nothing more I can say.'

Rachel closed her eyes tighter, hating herself for grilling the poor woman. 'Or was it his son?' she asked none the less. 'Is this all to do with David's son, Grace?'

'I'm going to put the phone down,' Grace said before Rachel could test the texture of her next silence. 'Then I shall take it off the hook. That's not the way I like to do things, but you're making this too difficult. You're making it too difficult for everyone concerned – and to no good purpose.'

'But a man might *die*!'

'Rachel,' Grace hissed back in utter exasperation, 'a man already has.'

Then she put down her phone. And when Rachel tried to call her back, four times, she had indeed taken her receiver off the hook.

8

On Friday evening Rachel came home late to find twelve red roses lying wrapped in the bathroom sink.

She and Matthew hadn't spoken since their confrontation over Nennius' story in the small hours of Thursday morning. Now they kissed and held each other. Then Matthew booked a table at a bistro across town, and was keen to take in a late film afterwards.

While Rachel changed her clothes the phone rang. Matthew answered it and called out to her. She came to the study, where he was sitting on the sofa, leafing through a sheaf of his own typed pages. It was the Director of the Centre, responding to Rachel's letter of resignation.

'I'll call back if this isn't a good time,' said the Director.

'It's never going to be much better,' Rachel told her, sitting at the desk. 'Anyway, there's not much more I can tell you. It's a purely domestic matter, rather delicate. But the way things stand at the moment, I can't keep coming. Would you mind if I just left it at that?'

Out of the corner of her eye she noticed that Matthew, poised above his papers, was quite clearly listening. She closed her eyes, regretting that constant surveillance under which he seemed to need to keep her.

'We're sorry to be losing you,' the Director said. 'People always say that, but I mean it. You know you can rejoin us within a year without having to retrain, don't you? We'd be delighted to have you back.'

Afterwards, as she continued to dress, Rachel began to

feel listless. Even without the trouble over Nennius' story it had been a hard week.

She had been in court for the past three days, embroiled in some spiteful divorce proceedings which had ended in two small children being summoned as witnesses. Then, just before leaving the office that evening, her mother-in-law had rung to ask if Matthew had come out of his 'funny mood' of the weekend before last. Rachel had spent twenty minutes trying to set her mind at rest.

Now she longed simply to soak in the bath and try to put her thoughts into order – especially her thoughts on what Grace had blurted out over the phone. But Matthew had already wandered into the bedroom, folding back the local paper at the cinema page. Rachel looked at it over his shoulder. She noticed that two short Italian films where showing at the cinema in David Nennius' street. She said nothing, but when Matthew eventually suggested the Italian double-bill she fell in with his choice.

The meal turned out to be fine. They felt relaxed enough after the first bottle of wine to share a second. Over the brandy Matthew became expansive, telling Rachel about the new project in which he was becoming involved: a piece of research funded by a children's shoe manufacturer.

Rachel took it all in, but as she listened she imagined him telling her, equally plausibly, that he found the work unbearably trite. She was accustomed to Matthew's pendulum-swings; she understood that he had to talk himself up. And back in the car, when he asked her about her own current caseload, she gave him noncommittal answers. Almost unconsciously, she had got into the habit of sounding as jaundiced about her own job as he usually sounded about his.

In the course of the evening neither she nor Matthew mentioned his writing. Several times Rachel almost did so. But a simmering resentment still held her back. One day soon, she decided, she would sit down at his desk and read his story for herself. *Then* she would talk to him.

As they walked down the slush-strewn street from the carpark, Rachel checked off the house numbers. They were arriving late, and most of the queue had already disappeared inside the cinema. David Nennius' house, a narrow but well-maintained terrace, adjoined it. As Matthew took money from his wallet, Rachel found herself staring down into Nennius' basement.

And Nennius was behind the window.

Rachel saw him for just a few seconds – at least, she saw his great feet and legs. Looking down from so sharp an angle, she could see only a fraction of the floor.

The curtains hadn't been closed, and the room was brightly lit. There were two large drums of wire just beneath the window. Nennius' lower body came into view, then disappeared. A moment later the same thing happened. Then it happened again. His steps were quick, yet graceful. Wearing the familiar tracksuit bottom and training-shoes, he seemed to be performing a kind of dance. And he was covering a wide area of the floor, for he made each of his appearances from a different direction.

'Come on,' said Matthew. A space had developed between them and the people up ahead in the queue.

Rachel took hold of his sleeve, mesmerised, inexplicably excited, and quite incapable of silence. 'Look at that,' she said pointing. 'That man down there. He's dancing.'

Matthew looked, then squatted and balanced on the balls of his feet to get a better view.

Nennius' feet and legs moved out of Rachel's range of vision. Suddenly she wished she hadn't spoken, that she hadn't so disingenuously called Nennius 'that man'. She felt that she had betrayed someone – but whether it was Matthew or Nennius or even herself she couldn't say. Matthew stood, took her arm, and moved her forward.

'He wasn't dancing,' he laughed. 'He had an indoor aerial in his hand. He was just trying to get a decent picture on his telly.'

But the image of Nennius performing his graceful dance alone in the bright basement wouldn't leave Rachel. He's there, she kept thinking during the first film. Whatever he's done, he's just through that wall. He's still around. And, whatever he's done, he still needs my help.

Soon after the second film began Rachel fell asleep. She

stirred halfway through, and Matthew suggested that they should leave. On the drive home he seemed to have lost his earlier ebullience. And, to Rachel's surprise, when they got into bed he just kissed her, then turned away to sleep.

Rachel woke at seven, and Matthew had already left the flat for a run. On his return he showered, said little over breakfast, and went straight back out to the supermarket to do the weekend shopping. An awkwardness persisted between them throughout the day. Rachel guessed that it had something, at least, to do with the fact that Alasdair and his wife were coming to dinner that evening.

While Matthew typed in his study, she spent the afternoon preparing food. Then she changed into a skirt, top and shoes which Matthew liked, and sat at the kitchen table, nursing a vodka and tonic. She stared at her beautiful roses, tapping her foot to the beat of her husband's music.

It wouldn't have been difficult, at that moment, to have wandered into the study and asked quietly, without irony, to see what he had written. But Rachel didn't make the move. As the vodka bit, she saw Matthew's writing as one more act of retaliation against the world. And she fancied – unfairly, she knew – that by reading it, praising it and offering her criticisms she would be joining him in his campaign against that world to which she really wanted them both to belong.

Alasdair and Maggie arrived at eight. They had spent Christmas at a ski resort and looked unnaturally tanned and fit. Matthew didn't emerge from his study until Rachel had poured drinks. When Matthew politely refused his whisky, Rachel knew for sure that the evening would not run smoothly.

He chose also not to provide a constant musical backdrop, where usually he did everything – even brooding – to the sound of his records. While the others sipped their aperitifs he sat at the dining-table, tapping a box of matches on its surface, smiling at no one in particular, making the occasional muted comment to Davis, who lay asleep at his feet.

Whenever Rachel passed his chair during the meal she was careful to touch him. But, although he didn't shrink from her, neither did he yield. No one said a word about work. They moved the conversation along with nerve-racking care from books to films to holidays. Rachel felt no better for having drunk half a dozen glasses of wine. She felt as if she, Alasdair, and Maggie were playing the fairground game in which you pass a metal loop over a contorted length of wire: if you so much as graze the wire, and activate a bell, you lose your chance of a prize.

But, as it turned out, the evening turned sour on account of something quite different from Matthew's sensitivity over jobs.

'You've heard that Rachel has left the Samaritans?' Matthew said at last, loud and sober, to Alasdair, who sat opposite him.

Alasdair glanced at Rachel before answering, then at Maggie. The women looked at each other, smiling different smiles. 'Yes, I had heard,' Alasdair said to Matthew. 'But I didn't think. . . .'

'Oh, look,' Matthew said, fingering the stem of his empty wine-glass. 'We can chat about this over dinner among friends, can't we?'

Rachel put her hand on his sleeve. He smiled at her, but she couldn't think of any words which mightn't aggravate him. The absence of music had become oppressive.

'Was it', Maggie tentatively asked Rachel, 'something that you've been working up to for some time?'

Rachel looked at the table. Leaving her hand on Matthew's sleeve, she said: 'Would you mind awfully if we don't go into this?'

Alasdair and Maggie started to chorus their acquiescence, but Matthew's voice rose above theirs.

'No,' he said. 'I think we should clear it up. It involves me, you see. It was me who asked Rachel to resign.' Rachel withdrew her hand. She saw that his fingers were quivering.

Alasdair touched his raffia table-mat. 'It's between the two of you, Matthew,' he said with an amiable frown.

Matthew turned to Rachel and tilted his head. 'The two of us,' he said, with a resignation that numbed her.

She stared across the table at Maggie. Her inclination under such pressure was to be facetious, to make dismissive comments, to burst into tears. But she couldn't do any of these things with Matthew. Their relationship hadn't been built that way.

'It's all right, Matthew,' Alasdair said carefully. 'Really it is.'

Matthew laughed into his lap. And then he stood.

Rachel looked up into his eyes. She wanted to say: It's true. It is all right, if only you'd let it be. But while she searched for the right words Matthew bent down and shook Davis awake.

'What are you doing?' Rachel asked, staring at the dog.

'I think I'll take this old brute for a walk,' he said with horribly forced cheerfulness.

'Oh, Matthew,' was all Rachel could say. 'Oh, Matthew. . . .'

And then he went, smiling his hopeless smile at them all.

They listened to him chatting to Davis out in the hall. They heard him closing the front door behind him.

Rachel blinked, refilled the wine-glasses, sighed, and went to put on some music. When she came back into the dining-room, Alasdair and Maggie were on their feet.

'You're not going,' Rachel told them, sitting again. 'Please. It's only ten o'clock.' She smiled. 'And we don't have to talk about Matthew, either.'

But as soon as they started, rather awkwardly, to discuss a mutual friend, the door-bell rang.

Rachel crossed the hall as quickly as she could on her high heels. When she pulled back the door, she didn't find Matthew looking penitent and keyless. What she saw first was the van parked across the street, with its engine turning over and its headlights blazing. Then she saw the figure at the front gate: Quinn, looking as if he wanted to move both backwards and forwards at the same time.

'Oh, it's David,' he yelled at her. 'I don't know what to do. I think he's dying.'

'Where is he?' asked Rachel, stepping out into the dirty snow.

'At the allotment. In the shed. I don't know what to do. He's just all hunched up. Sleeping with his eyes open. I can't get him to wake up.'

Rachel gazed at him. She had no idea where the allotment was. She knew that she was about to find out. 'Get back in the van, Quinn,' she said. 'I'll fetch my coat.'

'Ally, Maggie,' she said, grinning, as they came to watch her pull on her duffel coat in the hall. 'Would you mind holding the fort? It's a neighbour. An emergency.'

She waved away their own offers of assistance, then peeled off her shoes and stepped into her boots. 'I'm so sorry about all this,' she said, three times, before rushing into the snow, across the road, and up into the cab of the van.

Quinn then drove away so fast that she didn't have time to look back at her guests, standing nonplussed on the doorstep.

9

For safety's sake, Rachel knew she had to keep Quinn calm, but she felt deeply uneasy. She stared at his gaunt profile. He was driving without a seat-belt, leaning forward, peering out at the gritted roads, keeping just inside the speed limits.

She tried to think again of Nennius dancing in his basement. But all she could see was Quinn. She was sure that Nennius couldn't be dangerous. With Quinn she had no such certainty. This was, she had to admit, one reason why she hadn't got in touch with him. And now, as she swayed from side to side in the van, she couldn't rule out the possibility that if Nennius really was dying, then Quinn might in some way be responsible.

'Is there anything you can tell me?' she asked as they crossed the river. 'Anything that I ought to know, Quinn, before we get there?'

He didn't appear to hear. Rachel repeated her question.

'He had a bad night on Wednesday,' Quinn replied suddenly. 'I found him on the other side of town, sleeping in the van. After that he didn't leave the house again until this morning, about six. I heard him going.' He turned his squirrel eyes on Rachel. 'I didn't follow him. I was tired of following him, Rachel. All day I stopped myself going out and looking for him. But in the end I did go.' He swallowed, and glanced into the wing-mirror. 'I couldn't see the van anywhere. So I went to the allotment. He used to go there a lot, you see, before all this started – just to keep an eye on it, I suppose. And the van was there. Empty. With the engine running. . . . I found David in the shed.'

'But he was alive? When you last saw him, he was definitely breathing?'

Quinn nodded, slowly, as if he weren't completely convinced.

Rachel thought it safer not to press him. She considered saying: *I saw David last night myself.* But she wanted to say it only for her own benefit, so she asked instead: 'How much further is it now?'

'About five minutes.'

Rachel saw that they were heading towards the railway line, into the network of terraced streets which led down to the great flooded meadow on the western outskirts of town. And then she simply told Quinn, because it seemed absurd not to tell him: 'I read David's story.'

Quinn nodded, more sharply this time. 'Why didn't you get in touch?' he said. 'I thought you would have got in touch.'

He sounded interested, perhaps faintly disappointed. Rachel turned her head and stared out of the side-window. The façade of the old Infirmary looked unreal in the glare of the orange spotlights in its snowbound courtyard. What could she say to him? How could she explain, to him, the fears that she was only now articulating to herself?

'I don't suppose I knew what I could say,' she said. 'To you or to David. I still don't.' She looked down at her fingers. 'But the story ended so suddenly. It seemed unfinished. Were there no more pages?'

Quinn shook his head. 'Not as far as I know. I've looked. It's all on his discs.' He paused. 'The stuff you did read, though – what did you think of it?'

Rachel continued to stare out of her window. 'I thought it was terribly sad,' she said, 'and confusing. And rather beautiful.'

'*Beautiful?*'

'In its own way, yes, I think so.'

She turned to look through the windscreen again. They were travelling slowly along a narrow street with cars parked down both sides. The terraced houses gave directly on to the pavement. Quinn was shaking his head.

'Has David ever talked to you about any of the things in that story?' Rachel asked.

Quinn shrugged, then he glanced at her with an almost

hysterical smile. 'No,' he said. His face straightened as he looked back at the road. 'We don't tend to talk about ourselves very much.' He paused. 'But that woman in the story. . . .' He glanced at Rachel imploringly. 'Who *is* that woman?'

Rachel smiled. It was her turn to shrug. 'I'm not sure, Quinn. I'm not sure I know who any of the people are: Mary, the woman, William, Emrys. They're characters in a story. David's made himself into a character, too. They're probably not meant to be real people at all.'

'Oh, I don't know about that,' said Quinn. He had turned down a bumpy lane rendered almost impassable by the banked-up snow. They passed a single high lamp. 'William's a real person. He came to the house on Wednesday night.'

'Really?' Rachel looked at Quinn, intrigued, as he began to reverse towards a long barred gate.

Quinn nodded. 'He's been trying to talk to David for weeks, but David won't see him. It's something to do with David's son. . . .'

'His *son*? What about his son?'

Quinn shook his head. 'I don't know.' There was a frantic look on his face as he twisted around to assess how much further he could back up. 'The gate's locked,' he said when he had switched off the engine and was opening his door. 'I'll have to help you over.'

Rachel climbed down into the darkness. They were on the edge of the wide meadow, the flooded part of which was still frozen. During the Christmas holiday Rachel had twice come here to skate with Matthew. Behind them, running back as far as the railway line, were the allotments.

Rachel turned. Quinn was already crouching by the gate, beckoning to her and tapping his back to show her where she should place her foot. She walked towards him, took his arm, and made him straighten up.

'David told me that he'd done something, Quinn,' she said. 'Something he has to pay for. Do you know what he did? Do you know if he took a man's life?'

'I don't know,' Quinn whispered back, his eyes blazing. 'And I don't want to know. I don't want anything more to do with it. I just don't want David dead, that's all.'

Then he bent again, and Rachel stepped on him before swinging herself over the gate. She landed in a morass of mud, grass and liquefying snow. It had started to rain. The only illumination came from the van's tail-lights and from the snow itself. When Quinn was beside her, she took his arm. He led her along a short route marked by several sets of footprints.

He was prattling, increasingly incoherently, about the allotment and what he grew on it. There were rows of bare runner-bean canes, a heap of what was presumably compost, an area planted with greens from which the snow had been cleared. Quinn pointed her towards a large shed, made mainly of wood, with a corrugated-iron roof. Its hinged door was ajar.

Rachel shifted her gaze from side to side, away from the footprints to the pockmarks which the rain was making in the smoother snow. She realised, with some dismay, that she was looking for traces of blood.

Quinn had stopped walking. He continued to indicate the shed door. Rachel pulled up the hood of her duffel coat, watching her breath cloud thickly in the cold air. Then she went forward.

The snow had been beaten down hard at the shed's entrance. Rachel kept her eyes on that as she drew back the door and looked inside.

For a moment, raked by fear, she imagined she saw a huge man dancing round and round, his arms raised, in a dazzling bottomless silence. Then, directly beneath her, she saw Nennius' enormous form slumped inside his expensive overcoat.

'My good Samaritan,' he said to her, gently, without surprise.

And Rachel wanted to fall down into him.

He had closed his eyes. As her own eyes grew accustomed to the deeper darkness, Rachel could see a chaos of tools and flowerpots, and a dim white glow beside him. 'David,' she said, but she found that her throat was so full that she couldn't continue.

Quinn had come up behind her. 'Is he all right?' he shouted. 'Is he still all right?'

Rachel put out a hand to Nennius. To her surprise he took

it. The ends of his fingers were shockingly cold. There was no strength in his grip. A fast train stormed by, no more than a hundred yards away. Rachel cleared her throat in the silence after its passing. 'David,' she said, 'are you all right? Could we try to get you home?'

There was no answer. Quinn had backed off. 'What did he say?' he shouted at Rachel, louder than before, from some distance. And when she in turn didn't reply Quinn began to mumble: 'Oh Christ, oh Jesus God, please don't let him be dying. Please, please, please don't let him be dying. . . .'

Rachel felt some pressure on her hand. She could see Nennius' eyes again. They were narrowed, either in a smile or in pain.

'David . . . ,' she began again.

'I didn't want this,' he interrupted her. 'I didn't want this.'

'What did he *say*?' Quinn screamed at her.

'David,' Rachel said quietly, her mouth trembling in the heavier rain, 'for Quinn's sake, for my sake, could we try to get you home?'

Nennius let go of her hand. Already he was rising, stiffly, until his eyes were high above her. 'I didn't want this . . . ,' he said again.

And Rachel took one step forward, then she buried her face in his chest.

Moments later Quinn was beside her, beside them both, and he joined their embrace.

'I didn't want it,' Nennius continued to say, 'I didn't want it. . . .'

They stood together for longer than Rachel would have thought possible.

Quinn was weeping. Rachel pulled one of her arms free and encircled his shoulder. Her face was still pressed into the buttons on Nennius' coat. She breathed in the cigarette stink of him. Rain thundered against and partly through the roof of the shed. And Rachel felt, in those long moments, reconnected. She didn't want that circle to be broken.

But there was only one circle for Rachel, and this was not it.

She made herself step back outside, and allowed Quinn to lead the faltering Nennius into the rain. Then, remembering the white glow which she had seen earlier, she looked down. It was paper.

She stooped, and saw a sheaf of pages resting on a piece of sacking. She picked it up. And, as she did so, a small light object slid off it.

Rachel patted at the sacking, very gingerly, until her hand touched the object, then she recoiled in imagined pain. But it was only an edge of stiff paper. Gently she closed her hand over it again, eased her fingers beneath, and picked up a half-opened packet of razor blades. She folded the edge of paper back down, stood, and placed the packet in her coat pocket.

Looking then at the sheaf, she could see that there were lines of print on the top sheet, but she could make out none of the words. Outside, she heard Quinn encouraging Nennius over the gate. Quickly Rachel unfastened her duffel coat, placed the sheaf beneath the waistband of her skirt, then trotted after the others.

Quinn helped her over while Nennius climbed unaided into the cab, to sit hunched against the passenger-door. Rachel watched Quinn hoist his motorbike into the back, then she entered the van from the driver's side. By the time she was settled between the two men Nennius was already asleep. The cigarette smell of him seemed even stronger in the cab than it had in the shed.

'Christ . . . ,' Quinn was saying, between fast shallow breaths. 'Christ. . . .' And Rachel knew that he wasn't blaspheming. She smiled, placed her hands over her bulging stomach, and then began to shake.

'Would you like me to take you home now?' Quinn asked her when he felt able.

'Let's get David back,' she said. 'I'll ring my husband from your house.'

It took them ten silent minutes to reach the house next to the cinema. The rain had become torrential, melting the snow and flooding the alley behind the house. Nennius was still asleep when Quinn switched off the ignition and lights. The tumultuous rain woke the big man. He needed no assistance in climbing down from the cab, and led the way through the back gate, past the shed against which an abandoned bicycle was leaning, and then into the overpowering warmth of the house.

He paused at the foot of the stairs, clutching the banister.

'I'm sorry', he said, 'for all the trouble I've put you to. But you see. . . .' His voice tailed away and his face became contorted not just with bewilderment but also, it seemed, with a kind of amusement.

'Can you make it upstairs?' Rachel said.

'Yes. Yes, I can do that.'

'Then, go to bed, David,' she said. 'Please.'

He began to haul himself up the stairs. Quinn was behind him at once, coaxing him higher, fondly imagining that he would be able to catch the vast man if he should slip.

Rachel turned away. She sat on the mahogany seat next to the telephone. It smelt of lavender polish. The entire hallway and staircase, and what she could see of the kitchen and front room, were fanatically cleaned and tidy. She dialled the number of Matthew's flat twice, but no one answered. The grandfather clock opposite the kitchen door showed that it wasn't yet midnight. Rachel made a number of calculations as she wandered into the airy kitchen.

A bottle of whisky stood beside a bread-bin on the pristine work-surface. Rachel poured a small measure into a plastic beaker and drank it. Upstairs, above the loud hum of the rain, she could hear Quinn's voice. She was glad that she hadn't been obliged to go up there with them. She still preferred not to know whether they slept separately, or, as she now thought more likely, in the same room.

She poured and drank another small whisky, then tried to call Matthew again. Nestling the receiver between her jaw and collarbone, she allowed the phone to keep ringing at his end. Without moving, she undid her coat, breathed in deeply and removed the sheaf of papers from the waistband of her skirt. Matthew's phone rang on and on. Quinn came down the stairs wiping his nose on the back of his hand.

David Victor Nennius never knew his father, [the top sheet began]. He never even knew his father's name. . . .

Rachel began to leaf through the dampened sheaf. This time the pages were numbered. Quinn was standing beside her. She reached page thirty-eight, the point at which the narrative had been broken before. There were pages beyond this one. Pages and pages.

'Yes?'

Rachel started. It was Matthew's voice, coming at her from the telephone. The top pages slid away from her and on to the carpet. Rachel gripped her receiver.

'Where have you been?' she asked. Then she laughed, giddily, before he could ask her the same question. 'I'll be back soon, darling,' she went on. Quinn had kneeled down to pick up the loose pages. When he saw what they were, he began to flick through the sheaf which was still resting on Rachel's knees.

'Is he going to bring you home?' Matthew asked.

'Yes, I'll get a lift back,' Rachel replied. 'I won't be long now. I'll explain everything when—'

Matthew put down his phone.

Rachel hung her head. She was about to dial his number again when Quinn picked up the sheaf and took it through to the kitchen.

Slowly, but not quite unwillingly, Rachel followed him. In silence they sat down opposite each other at the table, the papers piled between them.

Quinn had started to read the new pages. After finishing each one he would push it across the table for Rachel. But Rachel was a quicker reader.

Within minutes she had overtaken him, and soon she drew ahead.

David's Story

1

One week later, at a wedding reception, David Victor Nennius saw the black girl for the first time. He knew neither bride nor groom. He was there only because he had helped to rig up the lights in the garden marquee. Standing at the marquee's entrance, sipping beer, he watched the guests move to the music.

A svelte blonde girl asked him to dance. He shook his head. She grabbed his hand and tried to draw him to her. Still he would not go. David had rarely danced with a girl. He had never slept with one. Although he didn't yet imagine that he was saving himself for the woman, he feared to go with anyone but her. On that night in the cottage she had staked her claim to him. And David had never considered that her claim could be challenged.

Then he caught sight of the black girl.

She was dancing, alone, in a thin dress which was shorter than those in vogue. David could not take his eyes from her slim naked legs. Whenever she twisted sharply the material would fan up, and David would glimpse the sweet outward curve at the very top of her thigh.

In the course of that evening David exchanged glances with her. It went no further. But, because he was looking, he saw her again soon after.

He was drinking in a pub. The girl was eating lunch with a group of older people. Beside her chair was a briefcase. In the brighter light he saw that the colour of her skin was closer to beige than to black, her eyes and cheekbones oriental rather than negroid. When she saw David appraising her from the bar

141

she smiled. Then she smiled again, in recognition. Her beauty was relentless.

Minutes later, she passed David on her way to the cloakroom. He looked away. When she came back he turned to watch her approach. She smiled. Again David looked away.

Won't you ever speak to me? she asked.

He faced her. I will, he said, perplexed.

Then he finished his beer, walked past her to the door and into the street.

It was a wet August. The sky seemed oppressively low and white, layered with thin bands of cloud like a succession of tidemarks. David knew that the woman was close. She was close and she was displeased. He felt that he was being pressed nearer to the ground. On several mornings he was sick before leaving for work. In the evenings he lay sprawled in the darkness of his room, sheltering behind his music.

It could not go on.

The black girl touched his arm as he passed her in the town's main street. He had been looking behind him for a bus. As soon as he turned to her, she dropped her head in shame.

It was early evening. Lovers were meeting in the entrances to the larger shops, then scuttling through the rain. The black girl tried to walk on.

No, David called after her. Wait.

She looked back. She had her hair in a red headscarf. The rain was driving against her face. I don't know why I did it, she said.

David smiled. Her loveliness appalled him. They went together to the pub where they had spoken before. Her name was Melissa. At twenty-five she was three years older than David. Her family had emigrated from the Caribbean when she was a child. After eighteen years her parents and elder sister had gone home, but Melissa, a graduate, had stayed on in the house, and gone to work for an insurance firm.

When she stood, saying she had to go, David guessed there was another man. He was wrong. Melissa spent that evening at a Samaritans training session. They arranged to meet again.

In the days that followed, David was intoxicated with

panic. He moved constantly in the shadow of the woman. The harder he tried to escape her, the darker her shadow became. She knew him, she had found him, and she would not let him go. But David was moving irreversibly towards a girl of his own choosing.

He took Melissa to dinner, and could do little but watch her eat, listen to her talk. Then they walked, her arm through his, to where she had left her bicycle. They kissed. David wanted those kisses. He showed her how much he wanted them. He wheeled her bicycle back to her narrow terraced street. They arrived outside her house and kissed again.

Melissa had left a light on inside. It glowed orange through the oval pane of glass in her front door. David looked to left and right before he followed her in.

When he came out on to the street again it was four-thirty in the morning.

Melissa looked down from her upstairs window, smiling at his refusal to stay until the day had properly broken.

It was warm outside, loud with the chatter of birds. There was an amalgam of scents in the air: woodsmoke, creosote, tarmac, dampness. David stared up at the window. Then he walked back through the new light to the home that would not be able to keep him.

In his bedroom he sat and smoked a cigarette, weeping for the first time since his mother had died. He sensed the woman's fury. He knew that she would exact a price. In her virulence she could, he felt sure, turn this beginning into an end.

Two weeks afterwards he moved in with Melissa. Three months later she told him with delight that she was carrying his child.

2

The news of the pregnancy numbed David. Beneath his own delight a deeper dread began to shift. He feared for the unborn child. He feared for Melissa, whom he now married. He sensed, without telling his new wife, that the woman was poised to rip them apart. He sensed further that the child's coming would give her the opportunity for which she had been waiting.

The months passed quickly. Melissa worked to the last. As an expectant mother she was beautiful, proud and confident. She looked to the child to complete her happiness. David found a better-paid job with a new firm, and Melissa suggested that they might one day start a business of their own. They made plans to that end. But no amount of planning could distract David from his main concern.

You seem so afraid, Melissa said at the end of the seventh month. They were sitting on her garden seat. What's making you so afraid?

Not *what*, David said, his face tightening. Not *what*. But he could say no more. He had never told her of the woman and he never would.

Melissa laughed. You don't have to be afraid, she said, kissing his sleeve. You don't have to worry about anyone or anything.

At night David would forget not to worry. When they made love he would draw back from Melissa, and search her face, her body, as if she had changed within his embrace. Often he would wake up alarmed, then feel Melissa's closeness and believe – for no longer than a petrified moment – that it was *she* with whom he had slept, the jealous unappeasable woman.

And when he came to his senses he would feel not only relief, but also, curiously, a sting of regret.

On the morning of the birth, the first day of May, David was out of town. By the time a message reached him, Melissa's labour was far advanced.

He arrived in the hospital ward, and a doctor took his arm. Walking David slowly down the corridor, he explained the complications. The child was being delivered by Caesarean section. David was helped into an overall and mask.

As he entered the bright theatre he was surprised to hear transistor music. It was the song that was playing, not the fierce metallic gleam or Melissa's welcoming smile, that made him break down. The singer's voice was familiar in a quiet unfamiliar song: a plaintive song of lies and dreams, of love and vengeance.

Melissa continued to smile. The instruments continued to gleam. A nurse and a paediatrician supported David as he staggered. They stopped him from falling. For several moments he heard only the song, which had erupted out of its former quietness. And as long as its noise continued he could neither move nor speak nor open his eyes.

The tumult ceased. A single guitar carried the song on to its end. The voice came seeping back around him, coaxing his memory, alerting him to an anguish which was inside him already and waiting to be felt:

> No one knows what it's like
> To be the bad man
> To be the sad man
> Behind blue eyes.

David looked at the table on which his wife lay.

A male voice babbled on the transistor. There was the cry of a child which David could not see. The nurse alone held him steady as the paediatrician went forward. Melissa's eyes were closed. The brightness in that theatre was more intense than any brightness that David had known.

He narrowed his eyes and she was there. Beyond the operating-table. The woman.

Less substantial than the other figures, she was casting them

145

all into shadow with her own brilliant light. She looked down at the child, down at the opened body which had brought the child into life. Then she raised her eyes to gaze at David, who at last stood alone.

He could see no one but her. She was just as she had been in the cottage. And he knew, for sure, that this was a woman who could be feared but not loved, who could take but not give. And he knew, from her smile, that she wanted everything he had to give.

The theatre fell away, the hospital and the ground beneath it and the sky above it were gone. All that remained was the woman who shone like the sun.

Her mouth was moving, although she made no sound. Her lips were set in that pleasing smile. David had never known such loveliness and it burned him. Again he staggered, his legs too weak to support him. This time no one came. He fell to his knees, then he fell again because there was no surface to receive him.

He fell until he knew that the woman was all around him, and he in turn was encompassing her. He thrashed in the shock of her embrace, flailing his limbs in a dervish dance of despair.

I know you, came a voice, from so deep within him that it sounded male, like a voice that was somehow his own, *I know you, I have found you and I will not let you go.* . . .

Why? David dreamed of screaming back. Why? Why? For still he did not know why his own life had always been designated as a payment.

Only one word came from his terror and confusion: *Father*.

And when the word came from him the woman had no pity. She indicated the child born from Melissa, bloodied but breathing, wailing, a boy, and she smiled a catastrophic smile. David saw the depth of her vindictiveness. He saw her tormenting him with end after end.

Why must this be? David longed to roar. But again all he could say as he whirled and sank within her and around her was *Father, father* . . . until kind hands were on him again and Melissa's smile was before him.

Melissa was safe. The child was safe. But David knew

that the three of them could never be safe together. He was weeping on his knees in the brightness of the theatre, in the dazzle of metal and the melody of a different song.

David reached out. His arms encircled Melissa and the boy at her breast.

Melissa gripped his arm. They cried into each other's faces. It was – David knew, without knowing why – a circle which the woman would shatter at her pleasure.

A strong hand was at his shoulder already. Above him a man was laughing, gently asking him to move, lest he should crush the baby.

3

Melissa chose to call the boy Art. David liked the name but rarely used it. Fearful of intimacy, he worked so hard that he seldom saw the child awake. He thought only of the rupturing of his family, of the end before the end.

What's going wrong? Melissa asked after the first year. They were sitting on their bed, half-turned towards each other. Why do you put yourself so far away from us, from me?

David smiled. He could only ever smile. Melissa reached across the bed for his hand. Try to explain, she pleaded.

This can't go on, he thought, gazing at the room, at Art's small bedroom through the doorway. The dread shifted inside him. I can't say it, he murmured. I can't *say* it.

Do you wish we hadn't married? Melissa asked him later.

No, he said. I've never wished that, I love you. . . .

Conversations of this kind could go no further. During Art's second year they ceased entirely. David and Melissa set up their own electrical firm. But the space between them did not close. Then Emrys fell ill, and quickly declined.

David spent silent evenings at his bedside in the hospital. He believed that the old man knew so much. He was waiting for him to share his knowing.

Why don't you go home to your family? Emrys asked at last, touching David's hand, looking down at the heap of books beside his bed.

David knitted his fingers. Because I'm afraid, he said, of how it will be when we're no longer together.

Why do you speak that way? Emrys whispered. You have all the love you need.

Love isn't enough, David replied, staring at the purple eyelids of the old storyteller, the man who had called him his little giant, his Albion. He continued, unnerved: I think you understand about me. Won't you tell me what I should know? Only you can make me understand.

Emrys touched his hand again. His fingers had no weight. Go home, David, he said. Go to your son, and be with him.

Two days later Emrys was dead. On the night of his death David went up to Art, now three years old. He spoke to him of the man he had loved, resettled the boy in his bed, then sat down and watched him fall asleep.

David stayed on in the room, stranded by death. His eyes ran from the sleeping child to the cardboard dragons suspended on threads from the ceiling. In the kitchen Melissa worked at the accounts, listening to the television. Several times she came upstairs. Each time, she laid her hand on David's shoulder and waited, saying nothing. Finally she came to say good night. And David, having wept at last, rested his head against her thigh, then continued his vigil alone. He dared not sleep.

But he didn't have to sleep. The images came, through the shadows and the catarrhal snoring of his son. They came. That night, David saw all that his mother had seen before him in her labour. And at last he understood.

He closed his eyes as dawn broke. Then he stood, plucked at the curtain, and saw a dim light above the roofs of the terrace opposite. I am the son of the sky, he thought. And, after so many years, he knew what that meant. He knew that he would dance before his time. And he knew, too, glancing down at his child, that there would be more than one end.

He went into his own bedroom. Melissa's eyes met his. He sat beside her and took both her hands. He wished with all of himself that this could have been a beginning. Melissa kissed him. We can go on? she asked. Can't we?

Yes, lied David. And they duly moved into the house that Emrys had left them, with its dark furniture, its wonderful books, and the anguish that awaited them all.

For three years the new firm flourished. David tried not to live in fear.

Often he took the boy to the allotment, to play while he

worked old Emrys's earth. On a bright October afternoon, Art came to him with a picture postcard from the allotment shed. Daddy, he said, offering it. Who is this? It was a photo of a painting: a naked man, standing with outstretched arms before a burst of light. His hair was fair like David's own, his eyes sad but resolute. He was immense, splendid, divinely human. David turned the card over. *The Dance of Albion*, said the print in one corner, *by William Blake*. But most of the back of the card was filled with a verse, written in Emrys's large careful hand:

> Gods and dreams and men go west, in search of their own white island.
> Some of the gods are men who have dreamed. The island is always the same.

David looked again at this beautiful man, whose eyes seemed to be looking beyond his own shoulder, seeing the chaos to come. It was a glorious piece of work. And David was frightened. He handed the postcard back. It was your grandfather's, he said.

Is the man Jesus? asked the boy.

Like Jesus perhaps, said David, lighting a cigarette with shaking hands. He's dancing.

Art turned and went back to the shed. He took the postcard home, and fixed it to his bedroom wall. Several times David found him staring up at the postcard. It haunted him to see a boy of six engrossed in so subtle a picture. Each time he saw it, he sensed that anguish inside himself, waiting to be felt.

Why do you find it so interesting? David asked at last, kneeling beside him on a Wednesday evening when Melissa was at the Centre. He felt driven to give the boy a chance to say what he himself was so afraid to hear.

I've dreamed about the dancer, Art replied. He's dancing out of the picture, towards me. But the closer he comes, it's not him, Daddy, but you. (He looked into David's eyes.) He does look like you, I think.

The boy's lips remained parted as he continued to marvel at the postcard. David was close enough to smell the sweetness of him. He put an arm around his son. Perhaps, he suggested, I should take the picture down?

Art smiled, a small boy of six. But I like to see you dance, he said. You look happy when you're dancing.

Then David looked into his eyes, through them, beyond them. And he saw only the woman, her shadow, and the end.

The end before the end came on the next Saturday afternoon. It was the last day of October, David's thirtieth birthday. The family had been invited to a Hallowe'en barbecue at the Samaritans Centre that evening.

David spent the morning out on a call. He came home in brilliant sunshine. Melissa suggested a trip to the park with Art. They went in the van, taking Art's cricket bat and a supermarket bag full of practice golf-balls.

Each took a turn to bat, standing in front of a tree, swatting at the hail of balls thrown by the other two. Noise billowed from the football stadium close by. Breathless, they wandered up to the children's play-area. There were several others inside the wire-mesh fencing, and some pigeons worrying at a split bag of bread. Art asked David to spin him fast on the roundabout.

Melissa stood aside, playing with a buckle on the front of her dungarees, enjoying Art's laughter. David saw her without being seen. There was a sombre look to her that hadn't been there when they had met. She was, if anything, lovelier than she had been seven years before. But her beauty had acquired a different sheen, partly solemn, almost apologetic.

More children came to the play area, frightened away the pigeons, and left. Just outside, a man held up a stick for his dog to jump at. Then, beyond the public convenience, which was some hundred yards away, the crowd from the football match started to spill along the main road. Art was impressed by the sudden shoals of people, many of them resplendent in the blue and white of the town's team.

David sat on the stationary roundabout beside him, watching

them pass. He promised to take his son, soon, to see a game. Melissa came to sit with them. Although the sunlight was failing, it was still warm. David stretched out a leg, pressed down his foot, and scooted the roundabout into motion.

This time he didn't work up much speed. Melissa clung to one of his arms and Art, less tensely, to the other. As their three heads touched for a moment, David closed his eyes and wished that they never had to stop. But when the roundabout was almost stationary again Art spoke. I have to go to the toilet, he said.

Melissa asked if he could wait until they reached home. He said he could not. David pointed across at the public convenience, beside which he had parked the van on arriving. Go on, he said when the boy hesitated. We won't move from here. We can see you.

Art skipped off the roundabout, left the play area and walked to the brick building by the roadside. David and Melissa watched him go inside. They laughed at him and waved.

David kept watching the entrance. He spoke briefly to Melissa, of work and of the Hallowe'en barbecue. The boy did not reappear. David jumped off the roundabout. He strode across the grass, breaking into a trot as he approached the convenience.

Graffiti covered the walls of the dank entrance-corridor. Names, addresses, slogans, accusations. At the turning into the toilet area there was an aerosol sketch of a flaccid penis and two bulbous testicles. The smell of faeces and disinfectant was so pestilential that David inhaled only through his mouth. The tiled floor was dark with wet, holding shallow puddles. Water began to flush into the five chipped urinals.

Above the noise of the water David barely heard the whimper to his right.

In the dim artificial light he could not see his son. The door to each of the three cubicles was closed. He heard the whimper again. A small grunt of pleasure. A man's noise. It wasn't the noise of a boy.

A roar shook itself loose deep inside David. Art! he breathed, pushing the door of the first cubicle. It fell back into emptiness.

The same happened with the second door. The roar was rising inside him: too mighty ever to emerge in sound alone. Art! *Art!* He nudged the third door, and it ricocheted back at him off the knee of a seated man.

But David had seen.

He wedged his head and shoulders inside the cubicle and there below him was the back of his kneeling son.

The seated man – no older perhaps than David, ruddy-faced from drink, wearing a donkey jacket and a pair of greasy check trousers which were opened at the fly – was holding Art's head, by the hair, against his groin.

His own head was tilted back in a kind of exultation. He must have felt the thud of the door against his knee, but seemed oblivious.

David eased himself into the cubicle. He wrapped his right hand around the man's throat. Let him go, he said calmly. Let him go, let him go. . . .

The man gaped up, grinning lopsidedly. At once he released the boy, who scrambled to his feet spitting, rubbing at his face, and exposing to David's view the man's rapidly wilting penis. Daddy . . . , he began to say.

It's all right, David murmured, arching his body, so that Art could squeeze past him out of the cubicle. It's all right now, my darling. . . . Then he took his hand from the man's throat and followed his son into the urinal area.

He kneeled on the sodden floor and searched the boy's face. There was a red mark on his freckled cheek, where the man had been pressing himself. Only that. His eyes were wide, tearful. Neither he nor David could say a word. There was silence behind them in the cubicle.

David took his son in his arms and held him. Then he led him out of the building. Melissa was already approaching, frowning, carrying the cricket bat and the bag of balls.

Go to your mother, David said.

He watched the boy run to Melissa. When he saw them safely together, he turned and went back to the fetor, and to the darkness which was, he knew, the shadow of the woman.

5

The man had staggered out of the cubicle.

David saw a bottle protruding from his donkey-jacket pocket. The man panted. When his eyes met David's, he tried to grin.

David went to him, closed his hand around his throat, and lifted him on to the tips of his toes. Tightening his grip, he forced him back and pinned him to the far wall. Already he had formed a fist with his free hand.

With the first blow, aimed into the undefended centre of the man's face, he shattered his nose. The second and third punches rendered him unconscious.

David allowed him to droop. His bloodied head brushed against David, who took one step back. The man scissored to the floor, landing on and smashing the bottle in his pocket. David watched, impassive.

Quickly the man came round. He rolled his head, moaned, gasped, spat out blood charged with gobbets of phlegm.

David stood over him, breathing fast and shallow. He turned away, crossed to the urinals and flexed his fingers. The man was trying to raise himself, as the liquor from the broken bottle oozed out dark and thin beneath him. He had started to cry. David knew what was expected of him. He turned.

He wanted to crush the life out of the man. He knew exactly what he wanted. He stood motionless before the whimpering and the incoherent prayers. He was standing in the woman's shadow. She had led him to this moment. She had guided him to the brink of the end before the end. She had set this nameless creature before him to be killed. He knew, and he stepped closer.

He bent down, his own face contorted by the fear of what he was about to do. The silent roar within him was a ball of fire, scorching his throat and blinding him from the inside.

He reached for the man's hair, drew up his head a short way and rammed his face into the tiles. When he did it again, the man stopped mewling.

David stood. He heard a voice at the entrance. It was Melissa, imploring him to come out.

But he didn't go out. The ball behind his face was spinning faster and faster, shedding a brilliant light through the building's interior. He knew that the woman was here, with him and with the man. The three of them were indistinguishable. And he was no longer prepared to resist her.

With water cascading again into the five urinals, David hoisted the man's limp but still living body against the wall.

Dazzled, deafened, he closed his hands around the man's neck. And he kept his hands there until the man was dead. Then he turned.

Melissa was standing before the light of the entrance. Her open mouth was loud with silence. She was holding back Art with one hand, preventing him from seeing. But she had seen. She herself had seen.

David – with a dead man heaped at his feet and the roar inside him spent – searched her face. What he saw was worse than death. For he saw in her lovely eyes the loss of all the love in his life, yet he could see himself going on from this end as if it had been a beginning. He knew then that this was only the end before the end.

Is anyone outside? he whispered. And it was only after speaking that he understood why he had asked.

Melissa put her hand over her mouth, stared, then led the boy away. David followed them into the open, looking about him, teeming with his crime. He did not want the body to be found in that place. Too many people had seen him in the park that afternoon. Far too many.

Melissa, holding Art's hand, walked slowly down the main road.

David looked to right and left. There were cars but no one on foot. The van stood at an angle that allowed him to load in the body without being seen from the road. Then he took his plaster-bucket into the convenience and sluiced away the bloodstains. The woman had made it so easy for him. She hadn't wanted it to be difficult, because she wanted him to go on from this. It was the going on, he knew, that would be so hard.

He locked the back doors, climbed into the cab, and lit a cigarette. Tuning the radio into a sports programme, he could see his wife and son in the distance. Step by measured step, they were walking to where he would never be able to reach them.

He turned out on to the main road and drove to the allotment. David knew that he was doing the woman's bidding. He was doing it so that he might suffer, endlessly, the deprivation of everything he valued.

A crimson sun hung above the allotments. Half a dozen men were putting away their gardening tools. Soon they would be gone. The woman would not let them stay. David smoked cigarettes, staring at the sunset over the meadow. Then he took his spade, and dug into earth he had turned only days before.

He dug until the fireball sun had long disappeared. As he dug he dreamed that he was entering the inner island, that dread island of Albion which would always keep his secret. The hole that he made alongside the shed was deeper than it needed to be. There would be no discovery. He could trust the woman; he was safe with the darker island. In that way at least, he knew he was unassailable.

He took matting from the shed and wrapped the nameless corpse. Then, slowly, he completed the burial. He prayed when he had finished, standing in the beam of his van's headlights. Finally he covered the disturbed earth by moving his heap of compost. No one was near. Only she, and the man he had killed, safe inside her shadow, a part of her now for ever. When it was over, he did not pause to look back as he left.

He drove without hope to the house. Melissa and Art had gone. David washed himself, cleaned out the van, then left for the barbecue. He arrived during a firework display. Until it finished he could approach neither Melissa nor Art. But he watched their faces across the fire. When they came together at last the stunned Melissa said nothing.

They drove back separately: David in his van, Melissa and Art in her car. David stopped to buy whisky and drank half the bottle before reaching home. Crossing the lawn, he looked up and saw the light at Art's window. Melissa was sitting at the kitchen table, still in her coat, attempting not to cry.

Tell me what happened before you killed him, she said. Then tell me what in God's name you did afterwards.

David told her, steadily, what she had asked to know. Almost at once she wept, but she made him go on to the end. He lit a cigarette only when he had finished.

Why didn't you leave the body? she asked, hushed, incredulous. Why didn't you come away with us?

David clutched the edge of the sink behind him. He gazed at the far wall, at the pot-plant whose tendrils had climbed unaided towards and then past the highest spotlight.

Too many people saw me in the park, he said. And the crowds on the road. Drivers. I would have been connected.

She wept harder.

David drew on his cigarette.

Melissa shook her head with contempt.

Then he took a single step towards her. And she screamed so loudly that the echo of her scream never completely died within him.

6

Melissa left David. She hadn't stopped loving him. She made it clear that she didn't blame him. She left because she couldn't go on living with both David and the knowledge that he had killed.

Because there was really no other way, she took the boy.

They left within a month of the killing. David sat at the kitchen table, pressing his fingertips together. His head was light from all the words he had spoken, heavy with those that could never be said.

I love you, Melissa said for the last time, standing in tears at the kitchen doorway.

David raised his head and smiled. Behind her Art was waiting, dressed in a duffel coat, holding a black bin-liner stuffed with toys and books. His freckled face looked so unsure. David kneeled before him, held him, and kissed his forehead.

You can always come back, he said – to them both – before releasing the boy.

Then he listened from the kitchen to the sound of them leaving. When he went upstairs to the boy's room, the postcard was still there. *This is all that's left*, the dancer's gesture told him. *All you can do now is wait.*

7

For ten remorse-filled years David waited. With each year his guilt grew harder to bear.

In waiting to be called, he severed almost every thread which connected him with his own blighted family. Melissa wrote to him, often, from the north of the island. He never replied. In time she married again. After that, David stopped opening her letters before destroying them.

He worked, he drank, he read again and again the books which had once belonged to Emrys. He passed his life in a limbo between the two islands, not quite dead yet not quite alive. Often he stood before the postcard, envying the dancer, imagining the happiness when he himself would hear the call.

His torment continued. Although the woman would not call him, she allowed him no respite. She stopped him from giving love and from taking it, lest for a second time he should fail in his duty to her. And year by year David learned to feel passion for her and her alone. He longed to be received by her. He dreamed of the release that he would only, ever, find within her – when the whole of him would pass into the white silence of Albion.

But when nine years had passed he believed that there could be a different end.

On the morning after the ninth anniversary of the killing, he found at the allotment a vagrant, sleeping alive in that place of the dead. He took the vagrant into his home, nurtured him, shared what life he had with him, in the delusion that this was a new beginning.

He dreamed that the woman had relented, that she had kindled a life from a death – conjured for him the opportunity to atone, to undo what damage had been done.

But the vagrant was no nameless man reborn. His coming was the mark of no new beginning. And when David awoke to the truth of this the woman spoke at last.

David heard her through the song he had first heard on the day of his son's birth. *I know you*, she said, with perfect clarity. *I know you, I have found you, and I will not let you go.*

And immediately the roar began to rise in him again.

Yet the sound of the woman had made him afraid. Too late, he feared he was not ready. He craved more time to make himself ready.

Above all he needed time to talk. Never before had he felt so eager to talk, to say at last what was clamouring inside him to be said – about the end before the end. The woman, however, who was within him and all around him, allowed no conversation, no confession.

Instead of talking she made him write. He wrote so that afterwards his story would be understood. As he wrote, the pattern came clearer. Day by day his fear fell away, and he knew himself to be coming closer to Albion.

When the story was finished – beginning, middle and end – David knew that he would never be readier. This was the true end, as he had imagined it so often, standing in front of the postcard, anticipating the happiness.

Taking his story, he went westward into the darkness. *This is the right way to be coming*, he told himself. *The only way.* The roar was rising higher in him, his penis was quickening. And the island shifted beneath him, the inner isle in which there can be no beginnings.

In his head there was chaos. A babble of voices. William, Melissa, Mary, Emrys, Art, the nameless man from the end before the end – all talking, all raving. Yet to David it was as if everything they'd ever said before had been a kind of raving, as if *this* alone had meaning.

He came to the place. The only place. The gateway. The voices between his ears had turned into fragments of a song. He closed his eyes; the pain and poignancy of the song were so hard to bear. But when he looked again he heard through the tumult the voice of the splendid woman, commanding and clear.

David, was what she said.

Just his name. And David felt already that she had emptied him out, and filled him with herself.

Then there was brightness. The area around his heap and shed was floodlit bright. He knew that she was there, at the source of the light, waiting: the woman who had drawn him so far. Within her was the nameless man.

It was warm on his own bare earth. He felt the vacuum beneath his feet, and through the vacuum he felt the warmth of the man within. Quickly he removed his clothes, folded them and laid them on the high heap. The tumult of voices broke loose again in his head, so beautifully tuneful. He shimmered. He could scarcely keep still. The roar was high in him now.

He stood upon the heap. The light felt good against his flesh. This was the gateway. This was the place to which they had been drawn, the sons of the sky throughout the ages. He narrowed his eyes. There, before him, was the richest fortress, and its door was open.

Pulverised by the light, at first he could not enter. The fortress seemed crowded with the woman – a single woman with countless smiling faces ranged about its inner walls. But already she was taking possession of him.

Already he was dancing slowly into brighter light, his head high, his arms outstretched. And once inside he threw back his head, blinked up, his penis burning hard. Hands touched his shoulders. She pressed him to his knees. Then she put herself beneath him. As he fell forward, she embraced him and she smelt sweet. David wept. The roar was in his mouth, her tongue was at his eyes. And, although he was with her still he could not gauge the completeness of her beauty or its complementary hideousness. He opened his mouth to roar.

But something powerful inside him prevented the roaring. Instead he gave to the woman all that was in him to give. And she took. He felt the opening out as he entered her. He was inside, the blood cascading. Then the tumult ceased, and there was silence.

She was moving for them both, just as he had known she would. Her lips brushed his cheek. Her fine hair streamed into his mouth.

At last he could see her face. Hideous, lovely, hideous again. A *man's* face in its hideousness, smothered in its own gore, a face which David knew, from the end before the end, smiling now, and drawing him ever deeper.

I know you, the face whispered in its exultation, *I have found you, and I will not let you go. . . .*

You're mine, the woman breathed at the moment he spent himself. There was neither warmth nor menace in the way that she said it.

She was all around him. He passed through to the other side of her and at last he was entirely safe. In Albion. The purest blaze of sepulchral white was there, whether his eyes were closed or open.

Gods and dreams and men go west, in search of their own
white island.
Some of the gods are men who have dreamed. The island
is always the same.

Standing alone, David raised his arms and stretched them wide. He was moving in the way that the woman had moved beneath him, a gentle rhythmic rocking, back and forth, back and forth, until his feet began to take steps of their own. Graceful steps, steps which could never be taught, leading his body through majestic sweeping circles.

This was the only Dance. His son had seen it in his dreams: the joy that came from the dancing of this Dance. Whirling deeper into the silent whiteness, David scoured away the guilt and the grief and the loneliness, until all that remained was pure love.

PART THREE

1

Rachel finished reading and glanced across the kitchen table. Then she stood.

Quinn looked up, his face devoid of expression. He was still a dozen pages short of the end. 'If I were you,' Rachel almost pleaded with him, 'I wouldn't read on. The whole thing stops making sense at the end.'

Quinn gave a small laugh, polite but incredulous, then lowered his eyes and continued to read. Rachel held the back of her chair. *The end before the end*, she thought, considering the ceiling. *The end before the end*.

She pictured Nennius' great body, heaped up there above them. She guessed that she and Quinn had saved his life that night. And a part of her already wanted to celebrate: the part which believed that the crisis had been met and passed. In fact her deeper anxiety wasn't for Nennius now at all, but for Quinn – vulnerable Quinn, mistaken by the man he loved for the reincarnation of a murdered child-molester.

She crossed the kitchen floor and set a kettle to boil. The rain had stopped. A dog was barking. Rachel felt sober, wide awake – and afraid, for she had lied to Quinn: David Nennius' story *had* made perfect sense to her. He killed a man, she told herself, and she knew it was the truth. He took a man's life, then he failed to take his own.

She made coffee in two mugs and took them to the table. Quinn thanked her without looking up. She returned to the draining-board with her own mug.

A wall clock, showing midnight, ticked loudly above the cooker. On the far wall, beneath a speaker, was the climbing plant of which Nennius had written. The dog outside had begun to howl. Rachel put her hand in her coat pocket and touched the little packet of razor blades. Abruptly the dog's howling stopped, a door slammed. She knew she had to ring Matthew, but she didn't want to. She couldn't imagine the conversation they would have.

Rachel turned and looked through her own reflection at the bicycle at the foot of the garden. A woman's bicycle, its covering of snow hardly affected by the torrential rain. But she herself was soaked. And since it was so fiercely warm in the kitchen she took off her coat and hung it on a cupboard handle. Afterwards she eased off her boots, finished her coffee, then padded across to where Quinn was still reading.

With one hand he was gripping the edge of the table. With the other, its forefinger extended, he traced his progress down each page. He had read only three pages since Rachel had last looked. She realised, with great sadness, that he was reading each paragraph of the story's climax over and over.

Rachel wanted to put her hand on his pony-tail. She wanted to tug it gently and laugh. She wanted to tell him that Nennius' story was not just a suicide note but a means of purging himself. And she wanted to tell him that in all probability the danger had passed.

She stared at Quinn's pony-tail, but she said nothing. His finger had stopped moving down the page in front of him. *He took matting from the shed and wrapped the nameless corpse,* it said at the point at which Quinn's finger rested. *Then, slowly, he completed the burial. . . .*

Rachel raised a hand to her throat. *The end before the end,* she thought. And she knew again that Nennius' account of the murder had to be truthful. She felt certain that he had constructed the entire story to make a kind of sense of that one ruinous episode in his life.

Quinn's finger moved on. At last Rachel began to quake with the horror of it all: not just the murder and its abysmal circumstances, but also Nennius trying to write it out of himself, then driving west to the allotment with his razor blades. She wasn't sure how she might speak about this with Quinn. She wasn't sure she could persuade him, like Melissa in the story, not to think of what Nennius had done in terms of crime or blame. She wasn't even sure that she could persuade herself. Nennius, she had to admit, was by no means out of danger. None of them was.

Hugging herself, she wandered out into the hall and tried Matthew's number again. The phone wouldn't ring. Rachel presumed that he had disconnected it. The operator confirmed this. But she had to talk to someone. So, with uncertain fingers, she dialled Alasdair's number. He answered almost at once.

'Rachel,' he said laughing. 'Are you all right?'

'I'm fine,' she replied. 'I'm fine. Ally, I'm so sorry about this evening.'

He simply chuckled. 'You're at home now, are you?'

'No,' she said after a pause. 'But I'll be going back soon. I've been trying to ring Matthew. I spoke to him earlier, but now he's disconnected the phone.'

Alasdair chewed on this for a moment. 'Is there anything I can do, Rachel? Could I help in any way? I mean, can you say what kind of an emergency it is that you're dealing with there?'

'Oh,' she said, closing her eyes and smiling. 'Life and death, you know?'

'I'm concerned about you, Rachel. Maggie and I, we're both concerned. And so of course is Matthew. You're sure you're not in any kind of trouble?'

Rachel began to wish she hadn't started this conversation. 'It's complicated, Ally,' she said, and then Quinn stepped out of the kitchen. His small eyes met hers just for a moment. Then he turned and climbed the stairs, quickly, two at a time.

'I've got to go,' Rachel told Alasdair, before replacing the receiver. 'I'm all right, I promise. Everything's fine. Don't worry.'

She went to the foot of the stairs. 'Quinn!' Rachel called without expecting an answer. Then she called his name again, already following him up the stairs.

He was inside the first room along the landing: a small single bedroom. A bonsai tree stood on a plinth just beneath the window. A transistor radio was propped insecurely on a pile of magazines next to the bed. From the doorway Rachel watched Quinn stacking clothes on this bed. Then he dragged out a green rucksack from beneath it.

'What are you doing?' she asked, as he fed his clothing into the rucksack. He looked bilious, and he was moving awkwardly, keeping his elbows close to his sides.

'Quinn,' said Rachel, 'shouldn't we talk?'

He continued to load the rucksack, scooping up a pair of slippers from the floor and cramming them inside. He glanced around to see if there was anything else. The transistor went in after the slippers.

'Don't you think we should talk?' Rachel persisted. 'About David's story?' She hesitated. 'Surely this isn't the time to be going anywhere.'

Quinn knotted the rucksack's drawstring, pulled over the flap and secured its strap. Then he carried it to where Rachel stood and said: 'Excuse me.'

She stood aside, but only because she thought it would be better to talk downstairs. Next door, in his own room, Nennius was probably listening to everything they were saying and not saying. They went down into the hall.

Quinn dropped the rucksack beside his crash-helmet and pulled on his leather jacket. Then he entered the kitchen. Rachel watched him run a glass of water. He drank it with his back to her. When he finished drinking he continued to stare at the window. Rachel knew he was waiting for her to speak. She sat at the kitchen table.

'This story,' she began, determined to find the right words, 'I don't think David meant it to be the true story of his life.'

With his back still to Rachel, Quinn snorted.

'All right,' Rachel said with a self-deprecating laugh. 'Of course David isn't really a son of the sky. But the *whole thing*'s a story, Quinn. It's not necessarily the truth about the way David feels. Can you see that?'

Quinn turned. 'I can certainly see that,' he replied, holding his empty glass in one hand and flicking at its rim with the index finger of the other. He nodded his head.

Rachel smiled, wondering whether she might, after all, have underestimated him. He appeared to be a great deal more composed than she herself was feeling. Suddenly she could think of nothing more to say.

Then Quinn spoke, softly, quite calmly.

'I don't want to talk about what David wrote,' he said. 'I don't want to know it's all there, inside David's mind, or wherever.' He attempted, reasonably successfully, to smile. 'It's not the things in his story that matter. I just thought I meant something to David, you see. Not as much as he meant to me – I knew that. But I did think I mattered to him.' He shrugged. 'I thought we were together.'

'Yes, but look,' Rachel said, rising, 'I told you: he might have *written* that about you, but it doesn't mean—'

'Did he ever mention me to you? When you talked?'

'Yes.' Rachel looked away. 'No. . . . Look, I can't remember. . . . Possibly.'

There was a brief silence, then Quinn continued, frowning at Rachel almost as if he pitied her.

'I know David wanted to die tonight,' he said. 'And I can see, from what he wrote, why he didn't want to go on. I can see why.' He set down his empty glass on the draining-board. Rachel had no idea how he was intending to continue. 'It was because there wasn't any more love. For him. At least, that's how he saw it – how he sees it.'

Rachel shook her head vehemently. 'But it was *your* concern for him, your love, that saved him! If you hadn't found him in that shed, God knows what might have happened.'

Quinn shook his head back at her. 'It wasn't me who saved him.' He smiled again. 'When I tried to get him out of the shed, on my own, he wouldn't come. That was why I went to you.' He put his hands behind his back and began to rock on the balls of his feet. 'I'd already lost him.'

'But. . . .' Rachel took a sudden vexed step forward.

'My love doesn't matter to him,' Quinn said flatly. 'I've been realising that for a long time. And now I just don't feel right in this house. I don't want to stay here with him. It's not the right place for me to be.'

They stared at each other. Quinn's eyes had begun to shine. 'I'll drive you home before I go, though,' he said, still staring at her.

Rachel imagined Nennius alone in the house, and the prospect alarmed her. 'I think you're drawing the wrong conclusions,' she said. 'Wait till morning, at least. It's already after midnight. Don't leave him now.'

Quinn stared back at her but didn't answer. His eyes were wet, but all the jitteriness by which Rachel had known him before seemed to have gone. Suddenly Rachel sensed the night crowding in on her. 'David's been through a bad time,' she said. 'He needs you here – more than you need him now. You can help him to begin again. Only you.'

But Quinn had stepped forward from the sink and was already walking past her into the dimness of the hall. He slung his rucksack over one shoulder. 'I've been worrying about David for too long,' he said. 'I've got to do something else.' He stooped to pick up his crash-helmet. 'Are you ready, then? I'll drive you back before I go.'

Rachel looked hard into his face. 'You can't just go,' she said, and she meant it only as a statement of fact. She didn't believe Quinn could wrench himself away without a final confrontation with Nennius, or at least some kind of leavetaking. It didn't seem feasible. He had gone to too much trouble on the big man's behalf; and, as she herself knew, it was so hard to switch people off. 'You can't do it, Quinn,' she said. 'You can't go like this.'

'He'll hardly notice,' Quinn replied, misconstruing her meaning, as he turned towards the back door. And Rachel knew from the catch in his voice just how bitter this was for him.

She looked away. Such a short time before, she had thought Quinn might have been *responsible* for Nennius' predicament. They stood in that hall, six feet apart, and Rachel knew that she wasn't going to go with him. Whether Quinn stayed away for only minutes or for hours, and whatever effect it had on Matthew, Rachel knew she couldn't leave Nennius alone in the house.

'Can't I say anything that will make you stay?' she asked.

Quinn simply unlocked the back door and pulled it back. He kept his face averted. The cold air from outside seemed to be coming at Rachel in waves. There'll be nowhere for him to go, she told herself. He'll be back. He won't be able to keep himself away.

'I'll stay,' she said. 'I think someone should be here with David. But' – she almost didn't say the words, because the echo from ten years before was so loud – 'you can always come back.'

Quinn, on the doorstep now, nodded once. He rummaged in the pocket of his jeans. Rachel watched him pull out a calling-card, then offer it to her.

'I told you William came last week,' he said, swallowing hard. 'He gave this to me. If David really does need someone – someone who matters to him – then William might be the one.'

Rachel took the card without looking at it. She watched Quinn tramp across the snow. He didn't look back. The gate swung to behind him. Rachel heard him opening the back of the van and wheeling out his motorbike. He must have wheeled it right down to the main street. Then he started it up.

Rachel listened until the roar had been swallowed by the stillness of the night. Then she closed the back door and went through to the kitchen.

2

Rachel read the calling-card and placed it on the kitchen table.

For several minutes she continued to gaze down at it. Then she returned to the hall, kneeled on the carpet, and once again tried Matthew's number.

He was still unreachable. Rachel closed her eyes. There was something grimly ironic about this: Matthew usually disconnected the phone only when they were making love. She dialled the number again and again, drawing comfort from the repetition. She could see herself facing her husband when this was over, hear herself protesting: *I did try to ring you. I kept on trying. What more could I have done?*

In truth, however, she was glad that Matthew had placed himself beyond her. (Surprised, too, of course, since he must have been going through agonies of speculation.) If Matthew had reconnected the phone then and picked up his receiver, Rachel would have found it hard to explain herself. For she wasn't just watching over a potential suicide. She was also under another man's roof because she wanted to be there. She was there to reach an end of her own.

At last, confused and increasingly apprehensive, she rang Alasdair again.

'There's been a change of plan,' she told him at once. 'It looks as if I'm going to have to stay the night here.'

In the silence that followed, Rachel had no doubt what was passing through Alasdair's mind. Don't make this more difficult, she wanted to implore him. Please don't complicate this any further.

'I was wondering . . . ,' she went on, her eyes fixed on

the rippled glass in the front door, and the indeterminate street-light beyond it. 'I was wondering whether you could possibly go back round to the flat, Ally, and tell Matthew? I still can't get him on the phone, you see. I know it's an enormous imposition. I know that. But I just can't leave this house.'

'I'll do whatever you want me to do, Rachel,' Alasdair said slowly. 'Of course I will. But what exactly do you want me to say to Matthew?'

'Just that I'm perfectly all right, but that I've got to look after someone here, at least until the morning.'

'And he knows where you are?'

'No.' She closed and opened her eyes. 'No, he doesn't. I can't tell him that, Ally. Really I can't. It wouldn't be a good idea for him to come here. Can you accept that?'

'It's no hardship for *me* to accept it, Rachel.'

Her eyes wandered from the front door to the small framed picture on the wall above the phone. It was an old railway advert, showing a thoroughfare in Leamington Spa.

'The person you're looking after,' said Alasdair. 'Can you tell me what the problem is? I mean, perhaps I could come and relieve you, let you get home?'

'It's good of you to offer,' Rachel told him, moistening her lips. 'But it's too late for me to hand this thing over.' She laughed: a brittle, dismissive little laugh. 'I don't mean to sound cryptic, Ally. It's just that – oh, I don't know – I actually want to be here, dealing with this. I'd rather be here, now, than at home dealing with Matthew. I know that sounds dreadful.' She bit her lip. 'It *is* dreadful.'

'Matthew loves you, Rachel,' Alasdair said after the briefest silence. It was as if someone had cued him in. And, although he meant it nobly, it sounded so glib.

'I know Matthew loves me. I'm not abandoning him, Ally. It's nothing like that.'

But Rachel knew that it was, as a matter of fact, something like that. Although she wasn't abandoning Matthew, she was running away from his kind of love for her: that cool, asphyxiating, inward-looking kind of love which they had contrived for each other. A love which had come to have more to do with fear and pride than with compassion. For that reason, if for no other, it was vital for her to be apart from him on this night.

'I'll go round to the flat at once,' Alasdair said. 'If Matthew won't come to the door, I'll leave a note. I'd just like to know that you're safe, Rachel.'

'Well, you can rest assured of that. Really.' Rachel smiled down at her knees. Then she got to her feet. 'Thank you so much, Ally. You're being marvellous. I won't disturb you again now. I promise.'

She went back into the kitchen and picked up the calling-card from the table. William Meredith, a haulier, in Lancashire. *ANY TIME!* underlined three times, had been scribbled next to his home telephone number.

She made herself another coffee and sat at the table. For ten minutes she pored restlessly over the story's ending.

Although the woman would not call him, she allowed him no respite, said the first of two sentences that had clawed at Rachel. *She stopped him from giving love and from taking it, lest for a second time he should fail in his duty to her.*

And when Rachel came again to Nennius' last dance she felt uneasier than ever, for she honestly believed she had seen a rehearsal of that dance through his basement window two nights before. Somehow she had known of the capacity within him to perform that dance. It hadn't been a guess. She had *known* – from what she had already gathered about Nennius, from gauging how powerfully isolated he felt.

She stared up at the ceiling, longing for Nennius to rouse himself, come downstairs and assure her that his nightmare was over. Until she felt happy that he was safe on his own, she knew she wouldn't be able to leave him. And it was such a sombre time of year for a man to have to convince himself to go on living. The worst and bleakest of times, in a sad bleak country.

Rachel glanced once more at the calling-card. William Meredith. *ANY TIME!* And he wanted to talk to Nennius about his son – a boy who may, or may not, have been called Art. Rachel knew so little about the real Nennius. Before that night she had been with him only twice. And she knew far more about him from his writing than from either of their conversations.

But the conversations had left a mark. They had made her feel that Nennius was a man worth saving. And the story, grim as parts of it had been, strengthened that feeling. Here, she knew, was a man she could help. Here was a man who had sought out her help. She couldn't let him down. She couldn't short-change herself by letting him down.

But if she were to pull him through she had to know more. And, now that Quinn was gone, all she had was the card. She picked it up and held it in front of her in both hands. William, she thought. William.

ANY TIME! the card cried at her with its emphatic underlining. But did that invite a call at half-past midnight on a Sunday morning?

Rachel had no idea.

Still holding the card, she went back out into the hall. Instead of heading for the phone, she then wandered to the top of the stairway which led down to the basement. Very slowly, she descended the uncarpeted steps.

There was no light on in the basement. But the curtains at the street-window were open, and by the glow of the lamp outside she could see that this was a cluttered well-stocked workshop. A small portable television set sat on an upturned drum of wire just inside the door.

A tiny glass-roofed extension had been built into the wall which faced the garden. Rachel could see a desk in there, the word processor on which Nennius had typed out his story, bookshelves, a hi-fi system, and two walls smothered with papers.

She picked her way across the basement floor and into the office. It was tidier in there than in the workshop. There was nothing on the desk except the word processor, an overhead lamp and a slimline phone. Rachel switched on the lamp.

At once she saw that the papers pinned to the noticeboards were pages torn from books. She leaned forward and read the passage which Nennius had underscored on the page just above the lamp.

> Silent as despairing love, and strong as jealousy,
> The hairy shoulders rend the links; free are the wrists of fire;
> Round the terrific loins he seiz'd the panting, struggling
> womb;
> It joy'd: she put aside her clouds & smiled her first-born smile,
> As when a black cloud shews its lightnings to the silent deep.
>
> Soon as she saw the terrible boy, then burst the virgin cry:
>
> 'I know thee, I have found thee, & I will not let thee go:
> 'Thou art the image of God who dwells in darkness of Africa,
> 'And thou art fall'n to give me life in regions of dark
> death. . . .'

Rachel sat at the desk. The bookshelves on her immediate left were packed with hardback volumes. Their subjects encompassed history, folklore, mysticism, topography, and a number of studies of the art and poetry of William Blake. These were the raw materials which Nennius had shaped into his own story. Rachel looked around her at the pages which he had ripped from the books. Momentarily she felt as horrified by this monument to his vandalism as she had been by his capacity to kill.

She closed her eyes, and ran William Meredith's calling-card across her temple. She didn't want to open her eyes. She didn't want to read everything on those pages in front of her. She'd read enough – more than enough. She wanted to learn no more about the man who David Nennius wasn't.

When she did open her eyes, she reached across the desk, and picked up the phone. She did so because she wanted to help the real Nennius, but also because she was excruciatingly curious, and frightened, and because she really didn't know what else she could do.

'My name is Rachel,' she told the sleepy-sounding woman who answered the phone three hundred miles away. 'I hope you'll forgive me for calling so late, but would it be possible to speak to Mr Meredith? It's about David. David Nennius.'

'David?'

'He's someone Mr Meredith knows.'

'Yes,' said the woman, gathering herself, 'I know David.'

Her voice was light, melodious; the accent wasn't northern but neither was it immediately placeable in any other part of Britain.

'I've been told that Mr Meredith is keen to speak to David. That's why I'm ringing. I'm actually at David's house now.' She understood how absurd this might be sounding.

'You're a friend of David's?' asked the woman. She sounded concerned rather than annoyed or suspicious.

'Yes.'

'David's all right, is he? Nothing has happened?'

'No, he's fine.' Rachel closed her eyes, nodding. *I'm scared,* she wanted to say to this woman. *I don't want to be in this on my own. I'm not used to being this scared.* 'So is it possible to speak to Mr Meredith?'

'He's just coming out of the shower,' the woman said. 'But, Rachel, you might as well talk to me as to William. He was only wanting to talk to David on my behalf. Or, rather, on our son's behalf.' She paused. 'I used to be married to David, you see.'

'*Melissa?*'

'That's right.'

Then her voice became muffled. Rachel, electrified, couldn't hear the words but guessed that she was saying something to Meredith.

'I'm sorry,' Melissa said to Rachel. 'I was just asking my husband to join us on the other phone downstairs. Would you mind if we made this a three-way conversation?'

3

'William Meredith here,' said a man with a clear confident voice. 'And who is this I'm speaking to?'

Rachel gave her name again, then Melissa cut in: 'Rachel is a friend of David's, Will. She's calling from the house.'

'I see,' said Meredith. 'I see. So David has asked you to ring, then, Rachel? I take it he's there with you?'

'He's here,' said Rachel, still assimilating the fact that these two people were married to each other. 'He's here in the house, I mean. But he hasn't asked me to ring you. It was Quinn who gave me your card. You know Quinn?'

'Oh, I know him all right,' Meredith said ruefully. 'I came down last week and he wouldn't let me in – wouldn't let me into my own house, mind you. I drove all the way from the other side of Manchester, and he made me stand outside in the middle of a bloody monsoon!'

'Mr Meredith . . . ,' Rachel said. 'So you're David's landlord, then?'

'Not exactly, no,' Meredith replied after a moment's hesitation. 'Could we just establish where you fit into the picture yourself?'

Rachel turned her head and scanned the spines of the books and records. Meredith's question was simple, but she could think only of complicated answers, and she heard herself saying nothing.

'I'd just like to get things clear,' Meredith went on, not unkindly. 'I mean, you're David's girl, are you?'

It was so silent in that little office. A lie, even a white lie, would have ravaged the silence. Yet Rachel wanted to lie, just to make these people, these *married* people, treat her concern for Nennius with the proper seriousness. But she remained uncharacteristically speechless.

'It would be a relief to me', Melissa then said in her beautiful voice, 'if you *were* David's girl. I'd feel much easier, if he had someone.'

Rachel listened. She couldn't bring herself to say: *No, I'm not his girl. I'm a more or less happily married woman who has talked to him twice as a Samaritan, then found him in a shed on the verge of suicide.* Instead she said candidly: 'I don't know David well, but I feel for him. I think he's . . . remarkable. And I'd like him to feel better about himself. I've contacted you because I'd hoped you might be able to help me to help him.' She paused, blinked, and felt a film of wetness at her eyes. 'Does that make any sense?'

'That makes very good sense,' Melissa told her.

Meredith cleared his throat. 'Yes, all right,' he said, at least partially mollified. 'Yes, good. But what exactly do you have in mind? For David?'

'Well,' Rachel began guardedly, 'I heard that you wanted to talk to him.'

'That's so, yes. Are you going to try to get him to the phone now?'

'I don't think that would be the best thing,' Rachel said. 'He's had a difficult evening.' She knew that she had to go on quickly, before they started asking questions. But again she could think of nothing to say. Her eyes were fixed on the fragment of poetry which she had read earlier: *Silent as despairing love, and strong as jealousy.* . . . And she was immensely relieved when Meredith decided to beat out a path forward.

'Rachel, listen,' he said. 'I do want to talk to David. And I'm prepared to come down again – tomorrow if needs be – but I've got to have some sort of guarantee that David's going to talk to me. The last time I came, he took one look at me and bolted. And I've been phoning him, too, and writing—'

'Yes, yes,' Rachel interrupted. 'But, Mr Meredith. . . .'

'Oh, for Christ's sake, girl,' Meredith laughed. 'Don't keep calling me "mister"! It's "William".'

Rachel also laughed and, as she blinked, the tears left her eyes. 'William, then,' she said, her voice unaffected by the crying. 'Could I ask why it is that you want to see David? Quinn said something about his son. . . .'

Meredith sniffed. 'It is about the boy, as it happens.' Then he fell silent, as if he had overstepped a mark, or feared he was about to do so.

'Rachel,' Melissa took over, 'I don't know how much you know about David and me. . . .' The statement hung between them and turned into a question.

'A little,' said Rachel, breathing faster.

'We broke up very suddenly.'

'Because something happened,' Rachel said on an impulse, glaring at the torn page on the wall. It was neither statement nor question. She was simply trying to move closer to these people, to show them how much a part of it she had become. She was also clumsily trying to raise, and then perhaps clarify, the larger issue. But the silence on the line was humming.

'Something happened,' Melissa agreed at last.

Meredith made a noise in his throat. 'We don't', he said, 'need to go into that here.'

'No, please,' said Rachel. 'I don't want you to think I'm prying. Please don't think I'm prying. It's just that . . . well, I'm fairly sure I know what the thing was. The thing that happened.'

'David *told* you?' said Melissa.

Rachel bowed her head. She had to say the words. It was essential for her to speak the words. 'I believe that David killed a man,' she said in a voice that quavered wildly. 'I believe that he took a man's life. For completely understandable reasons.'

She felt giddy. It was as if the words had been providing all the stiffness in her body. She only just stopped herself from toppling forward on to the desk-top. When she looked up, the line on the page seemed to be reaching out to her: *I know thee, I have found thee, & I will not let thee go. . . .*

Meredith spoke first, softly, urgently. His comment was directed at Melissa rather than at Rachel. 'This is bloody ridiculous,' he said. But from the edge of consternation in his voice Rachel was learning what she needed to know.

'No, Rachel,' Melissa said haltingly. 'No. Please.'

Rachel was aware that, as far as this couple was concerned, she could have been calling from a police station or a newspaper office. But she didn't regret what she'd done. She felt satisfied, if only because neither Meredith nor Melissa had slammed down the phone on her. Nennius had killed a man. Grace had said so. Nennius himself had written a confession. And now this couple were tacitly, uneasily, corroborating the fact of it.

'I'm sorry,' Rachel said. 'I really am sorry.'

There was another protracted pause. 'Let's get back to Art,' said Meredith. He sounded a long way away.

'It's all right, Will,' Melissa told him. 'I can do this.' She paused, then addressed Rachel. 'It's about Art – all this; it's to do with our boy. . . .'

She hesitated. 'Yes?' Rachel whispered.

'When David and I finished. I brought Art here. Will had offered to put us up, until I decided what we should do. He was family after all, of a sort.' She sighed: a gentle resigned sound. 'But in the end we just stayed, and eventually Will and I got married, as David's probably told you.'

'No,' murmured Rachel, wondering what she meant by *family . . . of a sort*. 'But go on. Please go on.'

'Well, after I married Will, David wouldn't have anything more to do with me. With us. So Art grew up without really knowing his proper father. . . .'

Melissa fell silent, apparently to let Rachel make her own deduction. 'You mean,' Rachel began, 'you want David to get back with Art again?'

'Yes, I do,' said Melissa. 'Will does, too. But Art himself is the keenest.'

'I see,' Rachel murmured. 'I see.'

'He's had enough of us up here,' Meredith said with some of his original gusto. 'He wants to try living with his dad for a bit. It's understandable. He's young, he's curious – fresh out of school and bored rigid with sitting around at home all day. And he's got this idea that he wants to apprentice himself to our David.'

'It's important to Art that he should be with his father,' Melissa continued, 'although it's anyone's guess how long he

185

might actually stay. But as far as Will and I are concerned he's got the right to give it a try – if David's agreeable.'

Rachel realised that she was smiling as she listened. It was as if the walls and roof of the office had floated away and left her in a large bright space.

'That's all I've been trying to do,' Meredith added. 'Just trying to see if David's agreeable.'

'Yes,' said Rachel, sitting in that large bright space. 'Yes, I see. I do see.'

An elegantly appropriate solution seemed to be offering itself. *She stopped him from giving love*, Rachel remembered, *and from taking it. . . .* She remembered Quinn, standing in the kitchen, claiming that Nennius wanted to die because there was no more love. She thanked God that she hadn't told this couple about the Samaritans, or David's flirtation with suicide, or anything else that might have rendered him unsuitable to receive the son who wanted to come home, bringing his love, bringing himself to be loved in return.

'Rachel,' Melissa began again. 'We'd obviously be grateful if you could put this across to David. Do you think you could explain that it's only Art who's involved here? Only him.'

Rachel looked up at the glass roof, the silent tears still wet on her cheeks. All her training and experience as a Samaritan had warned her against neat solutions. To go further, and *contrive* a neat solution, ran against all her natural instincts, too. But this was an unnatural crisis, she tried to tell herself. Nothing about this was natural.

'I'll certainly talk to David,' she promised them. 'But, William, you said you'd be willing to come down tomorrow.' She took a short breath. 'How would you feel about bringing Art? Just so that he could meet his father again? I'd make quite sure that David was here.'

As soon as she'd said it, it sounded unexceptional enough. But when neither Meredith nor Melissa answered Rachel felt bound to keep talking. 'It's only a suggestion. You can say no straight away. I just think an actual meeting would be better – I really do – than any amount of discussion.'

'Oh, well, I . . .,' Meredith began.

'There's nothing to lose,' Melissa said before he could finish. 'Is there?'

'No,' Meredith answered. 'I don't suppose there is.' Rachel sensed that in this matter it was Melissa's feelings that counted. 'It's not such a bad idea. As long as you're sure you can stop him bolting off again. We wouldn't be able to get down until the afternoon, though. I've got work to do in the morning.'

Rachel nodded. She knew she had made a formidable commitment. But for the second time that night, with this second pair of people, she felt as if she had been reconnected, and she wanted to say something spirited, something to set a seal on their unlikely tripartite pact. Instead, however, she started to laugh and to cry fresh tears.

'I'm not David's girl,' she said, as if in explanation. 'I haven't known him for very long at all. But to me he's extraordinary. A good man. A good, extraordinary man.'

'I know,' said Melissa soothingly. 'I know.'

Rachel recovered herself. She was glad that she hadn't been asked to substantiate what she'd said. She had so little evidence to go on. In the end, she supposed, it all came back to the man she had glimpsed inside the story. But she couldn't possibly mention that story now. In order to reclaim its author, she had to forget all about the writing.

'So you'll have him there at three tomorrow, will you?' asked Meredith. 'That's when we can be there.'

Rachel glanced at the hall clock. 'Today,' she corrected him. 'Yes, I will.'

They thanked one another and said their goodbyes. Then Rachel's stomach began to turn.

The end of this was still nowhere near. There was still so much that she didn't understand; so much confusion between Nennius' true story and his own refracted version of the truth. Then Quinn came roaring back into Rachel's thoughts. Disillusioned Quinn: out there in the night, his possessions rattling around inside a half-filled rucksack. And only after closing her eyes on her fears for Quinn did Rachel let herself think of Matthew.

Matthew. The man *she* loved: alone in their bed, beside a disconnected phone, giving up on her. Distractedly she

187

argued the case for and against trying to ring him again. The argument took her nowhere.

She stood, and her legs were unsteady. She switched off the lamp and mounted the stairs to the ground floor. The dog was barking again further up the street. She felt desperate to sleep, but there was no sofa in the front room, and only wooden chairs in the kitchen. Rachel realised that it was going to have to be Quinn's room.

She climbed the stairs cautiously, trying to make no sound. The dog's noise seemed to be flooding the night. The light was on in Quinn's room. Rachel lifted the maroon duvet. The sheets looked pristine.

She pulled off her top and skirt and, without switching off the light, slid beneath the duvet in her underwear. Staring at the bonsai tree under the window, it was David Nennius' face that she saw. Phrases, words, scenes and events from his story came rushing back at her. And through the wall, only a few feet away, was Nennius himself.

Within minutes she fell into a deep sleep – to dream of a monstrous howling dog which was swallowing, one by one, every star in the sky.

4

Nennius woke at eleven-thirty on Sunday morning. The curtains hadn't been closed, but all he could see beyond his window was mist.

He raised his knees against the duvet, to find that he had his tracksuit bottoms on. He was still wearing the top, too. Somewhere outside in the mist a driver was turning over a car's engine. Nennius closed his eyes.

I shouldn't be here, he thought. This isn't where I was wanting to be.

He kept his eyes closed. Then he dozed. But when he woke nothing was different: the mist, the tracksuit, the fact that he was back in the house. Even the car's engine was still turning over.

Quinn, he thought. Oh, Quinn. . . .

Immediately he saw the younger man fussing over him on the night before, pulling off his shoes, covering him with the duvet. Then he recalled an earlier moment: Quinn pulling back the door on to a cold silent place of darkness. He remembered being huddled within that place, looking up into Quinn's face. And then, oppressed, he heard again the animal noise that Quinn had aimed at the sky when their eyes met.

Quinn must have got him out. Quinn must have brought him back, delivered him virtually senseless to this bed. Nennius remembered only the palest outline of that. All he remembered clearly was the roar that hadn't risen in him, and *her*, the woman for whom he had wanted to dance, the woman who hadn't been there.

His gaze flitted to the postcard above the fireplace on the

wall. From the bed he could make out little of the dancer's body against the burst of light behind him. I was in the right place, Nennius told himself, although he was saying this for *her* benefit, presenting his own defence. I thought I was prepared, I thought it was the end, but there was nothing.

Why had she not been there, waiting? Why had there been darkness instead of light, cold instead of warmth, silence in place of the tumult? Why had the roar refused to rise in him a second time? Crushingly, there had been only himself – the beginning, middle and end of him – huddling fully clothed from the rain, so unlike the dancer on the postcard, so pitifully unlike.

Nennius eased himself on to his elbows. As the dancer's limbs became marginally clearer, the car outside purred off into the distance. Nennius felt weightless. He imagined himself filled with nothing but the mist. He swung his legs off the bed, his eyes fixed on the postcard. Why couldn't I dance? he wondered. Why not me?

He stood, allowing his tracksuit to settle more comfortably on his great body. And he remembered a third person in the place of darkness. There had surely been a third person on the night before – at the gateway and after. An unexpected girl whom Nennius, in spite of all, had not been displeased to see. But he chose to let this memory slip. He had to let it go.

He stepped across to the fireplace, and meticulously he started to work the postcard free from the wall. It was fixed with a blob of adhesive putty in each corner. Nennius had no wish either to bend the card or to leave marks on the white paint. Using his thumbnail he prised it away gradually, leaving the blobs in position, ready to receive a different picture.

He raised the postcard in front of his face. 'Why wasn't she there?' he murmured. 'Why wasn't she there for me?' But the dancer's lips were sealed, his eyes fixed on the future. And, although Nennius turned the card through many angles, he could not make that dancer's blue eyes meet his own. 'I wrote it all down,' Nennius said, as if the dancer were disputing with him. 'Beginning, middle and end. I was prepared.'

But the dancer offered no consolation. *You presumed too much*, he seemed to be saying with his effortlessly extended arms. *All this is mine. It can't be yours, too.*

190

Nennius lowered the card, and pressed it against his chest. Then he turned, still clutching the card, and left the room. On the landing he looked through Quinn's open door. The bed had been made, the window was open. Nennius closed his eyes. He had pictured Quinn in that place of darkness again, finding the rest of his story, coming upon the packet which he himself had failed to open.

Soft insistent voices drifted up from the kitchen. Nennius descended the stairs and, drawing closer, he realised that the voices were coming from the radio. A song started as he entered the kitchen.

The girl Rachel was sitting at the table, facing him. She set aside the mug from which she was drinking and stood with an uncertain smile.

Her hair was down. She was without make-up and wore a classically cut pale-grey skirt and top. From where Nennius stood he could see one of her feet, and it was bare. He knew, as soon as he met her eyes, that she had been the one, with Quinn, on the night before. He couldn't forget those alert reassuring eyes. They filled him with shame.

He smiled, holding the postcard tight against his chest. When his gaze slanted away from her, he saw his story, resting in a neat pile next to Rachel's mug on the table. At once the strength went out of his legs. He pulled the nearest chair across and sat heavily on it. Breathing hard, he bowed his head and heard Rachel approaching. She kneeled in front of him, then laid a hand on his wrist.

'David,' she said in that rich surprising voice. 'David.'

Nennius raised his head and looked past her, through the kitchen window. The mist was thinning, and he could see the line of the shed's roof. He took some deeper breaths. The girl had kept her hand on his wrist, and was, if anything, tightening her grip. The soft voices resumed their conversation on the radio.

'It's all right, David,' Rachel said. 'It's over now.'

He glanced at her. She had, of course, read what he had written, read what he had failed to *say* to her. Noting her tender expression, he placed his free hand over hers and they stood together. He wanted to let go of her, draw away

191

from her, but he couldn't do it. He couldn't do it. They stood without talking until Rachel's face clouded.

'Do you mind', she said at last, 'that I'm here?'

'No,' he said, extricating himself and moving towards the draining-board. 'No, I don't mind.' Without putting down the postcard, he switched on the kettle, drew a cigarette from an opened packet beside it and lit up. Rachel came across.

'Why don't you sit down and let me make it?' she said. 'Coffee?'

Nennius smiled. He wanted to say: I'm not an invalid. But the look in her eyes stopped him from speaking. There was nothing he could say, now that she knew what she knew and had seen what she'd seen. He sat again at the table and concentrated on his cigarette. A new song started on the radio – a furiously fast children's song with distorted voices.

From Nennius' side of the table, the story was upside down. He expected Rachel to return to her seat, place her hand on the script, then ask what in God's name it all meant. The prospect cowed him. He knew he was still incapable of talking it through. And he felt then, with a mixture of exultation and alarm, the first sudden loosening and shifting of the roar. But when Rachel brought his coffee over she sat sideways in her chair, and simply stared at the wall. She tucked one leg beneath her. Outside the mist was clearing fast.

'Your husband,' Nennius began, remembering, 'he knows you're here?'

Rachel nodded. 'I phoned him. I hope you don't mind.'

Nennius shook his head. He sipped some coffee, looking at her, seeing the loveliness of her and regretting it. She'd remembered that he took sugar. He finished his cigarette and stubbed it out in the tin ashtray.

'Should I explain', said Rachel, 'how I came to be at the allotment last night?'

Nennius shook his head again, half-closing his eyes. He wanted to know nothing about the web of involvement he had spun. 'Quinn fetched you?' he said, his flat voice begging her not to explain the how and the why. He worked a fleck of tobacco to the front of his mouth, picked it from his tongue, and smeared it into the ashtray.

Rachel nodded. 'Quinn,' she confirmed with a thin smile.

'He knew where I lived because he'd followed me home once before, from the pub, after we'd talked that time. . . .'

Nennius raised the hand holding the postcard. His eyes asked her not to continue. The roar was rising again. 'Where is Quinn now?'

Rachel raised her eyebrows. 'He went out, on his bike. Around midnight.' She looked down. 'He'd packed his things.'

Nennius rubbed the ball of his hand across his forehead, screwing up his eyes. He knew Rachel was taking note of the dirty plasters which still covered the cuts on his knuckles.

It was easy for Nennius to work out what had happened: Quinn had read the rest of the story. He had read it all – beginning, middle and end. And what he had read had driven him out. How could it not have? And now only this girl, whom he had found in Melissa's place, was left. Just the two of them, and the roar that was rising. Nennius stood. He ran a plastered hand up the side of his face. 'Please,' he said. 'Let me drive you home now.'

Rachel looked up, determined and concerned. She had picked up a box of matches and was tapping it lightly on the table-top. 'You must be hungry,' she said. 'I could make us something to eat.'

Nennius took some time to realise what she was saying. She wasn't intending to go. Quinn had gone, but she was staying. Nennius turned the postcard round between his fingers, its picture side facing Rachel. 'I don't want to talk,' he said, and his glance dropped briefly to the story.

'You don't need to talk. You don't need to say or do anything.'

He smiled, even though the whole of him was quaking. I went to her, he thought airily, and now she's come to me. A good and beautiful girl in stylish clothes and bare feet. And he didn't have the resources to argue.

'I'll go up and have a shower,' he said, turning away.

She nodded back and opened the fridge before he left the room.

He remained beneath the shower until the blistering water turned tepid. Inside the steam he hummed tunes to stall the roar, to prevent his mind from running on.

Afterwards he shaved. And when he had finished shaving

he took a new packet of razor blades from the bathroom cabinet and carried it through to his bedroom. He put on a crisp white shirt, a navy tie, his best charcoal-grey two-piece suit, and the Italian black laced shoes which Quinn had polished to a shine. Before going downstairs he propped up the postcard on the mantelpiece. Then he slipped the packet of razor blades into his trouser pocket.

Rachel had changed the station on the radio and tuned into a concerto for strings. She was standing at the sink, washing the pans in which she had long since fried eggs, bacon, mushrooms, and tomatoes. She turned, and when she saw Nennius she gave a little gasp.

'You look splendid, David,' she said, but her smile couldn't quite conceal her anxiety. Quickly she looked back down at the frothing water and added: 'Are you planning on going somewhere?'

5

Rachel waited in vain for Nennius to answer her question. When she looked at him again he frowned, as if he couldn't understand why she had asked. He walked to the table and sat down.

Formal dress made a drastic difference to his appearance. The shave had changed him, too. Rachel had never seen him completely clean-jawed before. His cheeks had a red flush, his large eyes seemed prominent, even zealous. And with his hair slicked back from his face he looked as much as ten years younger.

Rachel dried her hands, then took the food from under the grill, burning a finger on one of the plates. Both meals had congealed. She laid them on the table, with apologies, and they ate to the accompaniment of a Mozart symphony. Whenever Rachel thought to speak, she was discouraged by the fervently absorbed look in Nennius' new face.

It was half-past twelve. Rachel had risen three hours before. To while away some of the time, she had looked through Nennius' complete story.

From the beginning she had been responding, at least in part, to the writing *as* writing. She had been seduced by the strange slickness with which it kept the pain at bay. Now she could almost believe that there were *two* real Nenniuses, both blighted by being *stopped*, in the author's phrase, *from giving love and from taking it*. The Nennius who sat at the kitchen table could surely be salvaged by the love of his son. But who, she wondered half-seriously, who would give and take love with the other Nennius, the one still trapped in the story?

She watched the big man pick at his food, then push his plate aside. 'Thank you,' he said, his eyes averted. 'Now I must drive you home.'

Rachel pushed aside her own plate until it almost touched the story. She locked her fingers together on the table-top. Although she would have preferred to postpone this conversation for an hour or so, she knew she had to speak. 'David,' she began, 'I've got something to say.'

Nennius didn't move, but within himself he seemed to be shrinking from her. Rachel reached across the table and put her hand on his. The fabric plasters on his knuckles were still damp. At her touch he recoiled, leaning back from the waist, and staring down at her hand as if it nauseated him.

Rachel wanted to rise and go to him, hug him to her. There was such an unnecessary distance between them. The phrase *silent as despairing love* came to her again from the torn page on the wall of his little office. Then a prayer flashed through her head: an entreaty for God to smile on what she had done and on what she was about to do.

'Quinn told me about Meredith,' she said quickly, tightening her hold on his hand. She felt that if only this physical connection could be maintained, then neither of them could fail. 'He told me how urgently Meredith wanted to talk to you. So I rang him, from here, late last night.'

Nennius turned his face to the wall. The symphony ended, and the room was eerie with silence before the announcer started to speak.

'It's to do with your son, David,' Rachel went on. 'It's Art – he wants to come and live with you. Here. He wants to work with you. It's nothing bad, David. It's a good thing. A really good thing, don't you see?'

Nennius drew his hand away with such unexpected force that Rachel was pulled part of the way with it. She stood, leaning across the table, her face only inches away from his. His nostrils flared while the rest of his face remained impassive.

'Art loves you, David,' she said, too loudly. 'He needs to be with you.'

'Loves me,' Nennius murmured as he got to his feet.

'Oh, David,' Rachel cried, coming around the table to him. But when she was almost upon him Nennius raised a forbidding hand.

'Don't come close,' he said, glaring. 'Don't touch me again.'

Rachel glared back at him. 'You're a good man, David,' she said levelly. 'You think there's no more love, but there is. There is. You've got to let people show their love for you.'

'So what are you saying?' he said in a slow, almost contemptuous, drawl.

Rachel looked into his eyes and only then did she fully understand what those eyes had seen. She glanced at his hands, and she understood that they had wrung out a life.

Gathering herself, clutching at the table with one hand, she stared into his chest, where his tie rested so primly on his pressed white shirt. 'What I'm saying, David, is that there's no need for you to die. Too many people want you here' – and with a sweeping gesture she indicated the room – 'on *this* island.'

Nennius' expression softened. He raised a hand and touched his scarred forehead, then he frowned, and Rachel wondered for a moment whether he was going to weep where he stood. But he didn't weep. He reached past her and picked up his story from the table.

Rachel stepped aside. She folded her arms in frustration. He was holding his stack of pages as reverently as he had been holding that much-vaunted postcard when he had first come downstairs.

'That's just a story, David,' she said, hearing the hardness in her voice.

He pressed the pages against his stomach.

'That's just a story,' she repeated, holding his gaze. 'Art's real. I'm real. Quinn's real. You know that. I know you know it.' She took a step towards him, scarcely stopping to think before going on. 'You can't give yourself to a woman who isn't there, David. You can't. Not after last night. You don't even *want* to! That's why you told Quinn about her. That's why you came to me – twice. Don't you see? Can't you see?'

Nennius turned abruptly and left the kitchen, but Rachel followed him. He descended the stairs into the basement. She pursued him across the workshop to his office, then she leaned against its doorless architrave as he placed his story on the desk, squatted down, and began to riffle hurriedly through the spines of his record albums.

'Meredith is driving down right now,' Rachel said to his back. 'He's bringing Art with him.' She saw Nennius pause at that, then continue with his riffling. 'Just so that you can be with each other again, David. You've got to see that it can only be good.'

Nennius chose an album, took the record from its pale blue sleeve, and placed it on the turntable. Rachel watched, feeling dashed. Nennius drew the arm across and set down the stylus at the beginning of a song.

The music began at such a high volume that Rachel looked left and right in amazement. She had no chance of making herself heard above the din.

Nennius seated himself at the desk, his eyes closed, his strangely youthful face composed. The story was in front of him. He had never been so far away from Rachel. She was losing him. She had, she knew, driven him off by telling too much truth, too soon, too incompetently.

She looked to one side, at the nearest page pinned to the wall. *Said Arthur, 'Is there any of the marvels still unobtained?'* Nennius' selected passage began. *Said one of the men, 'There is: the blood of the Black Witch, daughter of the White Witch, from the head of the Valley of Grief in the uplands of Hell.'*

'Oh shit,' Rachel muttered. 'Shit, shit, shit.'

She took a step back into the workshop, away from the noise. The strident rock song seemed to be running quickly out of the musicians' control. Nennius seemed comatose in his chair. His ridiculous response to her botched approach was making Rachel feel ridiculous, too.

But as she stared at his great guilty hands she told herself that it could have been worse. He might have tried to leave the house. At least he was still there. And that, in the longer term, was all that mattered.

She took another step back. The clock on the workshop wall showed one-fifteen. Nennius, his head bowed, looked as if he would never move again. But he was there. And Rachel wondered whether her shock tactics mightn't have

198

been misplaced after all. It was just possible that Nennius was actually making himself ready for the visit. But, whatever he was doing, Rachel had little to gain from standing by and watching him do it.

She turned, and without looking back she climbed the stairs to the kitchen, where she set herself to washing up the plates.

Since Nennius' music was carrying so far, she switched off the radio. But she was willing to put up with any amount of his turbulence – just as long as it continued to tell her that he was still there, where she wanted him to be, where he himself surely knew that he had to be. Rachel raised her eyes and prayed again, this time aloud: 'Please, God, let him want what I'm giving him. Please, please, let this be the right thing.'

Out in the garden the mist had gone. Apart from the trails of footprints from the back gate, left by the comings and goings of the night before, the blanket of snow lay undisturbed. A cat sat on an upturned cold frame just in front of the shed. To the side of it stood the bicycle, still caked with snow. And, early though it was, the low grey sky was already anticipating the close of the day.

Rachel leaned forward, her hands and wrists submerged in the greasy water. Thankfully a silence was coursing through the house at the end of the song.

Seconds later it was broken, this time by a restrained introduction, picked out on a single guitar.

Rachel turned her head. Somehow this piece sounded closer than the chaotic song that had preceded it. And when the singer's voice came wheedling in she raised her eyes and realised that Nennius had switched the music through to the extension speakers on the kitchen's far wall.

She asked herself, smiling, if he was trying to drive her into the alley. And at first she paid no attention to what the vocalist was singing: listening to the words of rock songs wasn't something that she did. But as she tipped away the washing-up water she caught a familiar phrase.

She paused. It was the song from Nennius' story. The song about blue eyes, quoted in the passage about his son's birth. Intently she walked across to where the tea-towel hung. This took her into a part of the room where the stereo effect was startlingly apparent. The song folded itself around her; a mournful song about biting back on anger, hiding pain, dreaming dreams and telling lies.

Rachel tilted her head. She presumed that Nennius was trying to reach her through the song. But when the quiet introductory passage gave way to an onslaught of electric guitars and drums the lyrics became less distinct and for her less coherent. Rachel dried her hands on the tea-towel and dutifully she heard out the turbulence. At last, after little more than three minutes, only the original acoustic guitar was left, paving the way for the last verse – a repeat of the first. And on the final phrase of this verse a second voice, pitched higher and more plaintively, joined that of the singer:

> No one knows what it's like
> To be the bad man
> To be the sad man
> Behind blue eyes.

Then it was over. Rachel pursed her lips. As the next song came spilling from the speakers she was on her way out of the kitchen and descending the stairs to the office. Yes, David, she was intending to say, but a song is a song and a story's just a story. And you've left them behind you now. They don't signify any more.

But Nennius wasn't in the office.

Rachel swept across to the amplifier, found the volume control and reduced the din to a hiss. 'David?' she called out, standing by the bookshelves, and then more loudly, with less self-consciousness, 'David!' She noticed that the story had gone from the desk.

On the floor lay the sleeve of the record that was playing. The cover photo showed four young men in a desolate place, turning away from a concrete pillar against which they had urinated. The only words, set small into a clouded blue sky, were *Who's next*.

Rachel rushed from the office and shrieked up the stairs: '*David!*'

When no answer came, she raced up into the hall, checked

that the front room and kitchen were empty, then continued on up the second flight of stairs. Without calling his name she flung back each door on the landing and looked inside. The last room was Nennius' own. Rachel entered, drawn in by the postcard which was now propped up on the mantelpiece.

She stepped through the discarded clothing on the carpet, seized the card and turned it over.

The printed legend confirmed that it was indeed 'The Dance of Albion' by William Blake. But underneath there was an additional note: 'Also known as "Glad Day".' And the written message was quite unlike the one Nennius had recorded in his story. *To Melissa and David*, it said, *on the occasion of your gladdest day. Congratulations to you all. May baby Art bring you only joy. With all my love, Emrys.*

Rachel, feeling as if she had been punched in the face, replaced the postcard and went back down the stairs. He had definitely gone. She had let him go. Standing in the kitchen, she had let him walk away.

In the hall she saw that the front door had blown back a short way.

She found that it had been left on the latch. She went out on to the doorstep in her bare feet, but David Nennius wasn't in the street. He had gone, and Rachel knew where he would be heading. There was only one place for him to go. Back into his story.

It can't end here, she thought as a dangerous torpor tried to take hold of her. I've got to go, too.

Out there on the doorstep, with the song about blue eyes roiling in her head, she remembered the bicycle in front of the shed. And already she was planning out the shortest route across town to Nennius' allotment. Only speed, not self-reproach, mattered now.

She returned to the kitchen, where she pulled on her duffel coat and boots. Tearing a corner from the top sheet of a wall calendar, she scribbled a short explicit note to William on its reverse side, directing him to the allotments. This she fixed beneath the front-door knocker, then shut herself back in the house. Time, she was only too aware, was spinning away.

She went straight through to the back garden and swept

the snow from the bicycle. Its tyres weren't as hard as they might have been, but otherwise it seemed quite serviceable. She wheeled it out of the garden, on to the chippings where, praise God, Nennius' van was still parked. Rachel guessed that on foot he couldn't reach the allotment in less than thirty minutes. There were a number of plausible routes into the west of the town. But Rachel, mounting the bicycle, felt confident that she could either catch him up or arrive first.

She had to feel confident. It stopped her from dwelling on what might happen if David Nennius got back to the climax of his story before she did.

6

Nennius stopped running only when he reached the end of his long street.

The lamps were on. It was raining. When breathlessly he looked behind him, he was looking not for Rachel but for Quinn, whom he half-expected to find running still, chasing hard. Only the darkness was there. And this darkness was the shadow of the woman.

He turned left down a wide road which took him into, and then through, the light industrial estate which led away from the town centre. Heading for Melissa's district, he pulled off his jacket and folded it around his story. He had to protect the story.

The Sunday pavements were deserted, the roads almost free of traffic. Nennius held his story tenderly in front of him, in both hands, as if it were a living thing. Now and then he broke into a trot. Mostly he strode, panting, with little in his head, as the silent roar transformed itself.

Soon he was among the narrower roads. Melissa's district. It would always be hers. He could no longer remember why he was taking so circuitous a route to his journey's end. *Gods and dreams and men go west.* . . . All he knew was that this was the right way to be coming. He saw the lips parting, felt the shifting beneath his feet, sensed the love that was waiting.

At the turn into Melissa's street two youths in leather were tinkering with a motorbike. Nennius checked his step, to make sure that neither was Quinn. Then he careered on, through the insistent rain, down the street along which he had wheeled Melissa's bicycle on that first mistaken evening.

He didn't look up as he passed the house. Melissa wasn't there. Melissa was hundreds of miles to the north. Melissa – dancing in a short dress at the beginning, the wrong girl. He had made her beauty solemn. She had screamed a scream that had never died inside him.

Art, thought Nennius. 'Art, Art, Art,' he breathed aloud. But it was just a word. A short word. On Rachel's lips the word had become a name. And she'd coupled it with talk of love, goodness, going on. Rachel had almost reached him with those words. But one woman alone could reach him now.

'*Art!*' Nennius cried on the track which wound down to the allotments. He saw the back of his son's little neck, he smelt the fetor, but he heard only the echo of a word. There was no son for him. No love or goodness or going on. He clutched the story tighter. This, here, in a place of death and discovery, this was what was his. The heat of the roar deafened him and blinded him, making him ready for the Dance. He felt his penis quicken.

The rain thinned. At the end of the track Nennius saw the first trace of light. He ran on, plashing through mud churned up by his van on the night before. He narrowed his eyes at the light flooding from his own allotment. The lips were large before him, the space between them wider as they twisted: moaning, gasping, mewling, weeping, a *man's* mouth momentarily, a mouth in the broken face of a man with no name. Nennius smiled. The lips smiled back, a woman's lips again.

Inside the pale outer glow, he threw back his head, walking on towards the gate. The rain had gone. The sky had gone. There were only rivers of light, torrents of gorgeous colour, rushing from her fortress. She was inside each particle of this light. She was the beginning and the middle and the end.

Nennius came to the gate, tucked his parcel under one arm, and hauled himself over. The light on the other side was ferocious. A vibrant light, bursting around him in reds, yellows, blues. It filled him with the need to move. He had never felt so weightless. Only his clothes stopped the light from drawing his roar and sweeping him into the Dance.

He stepped closer. Behind the cascades of colour he saw a

many-turreted silhouette. He felt her lips swarming over him, coaxing him out of his clothes, waiting to take the whole of him. But the fortress came no closer. He was beside a heap of his own making. *Gods and dreams and men go west, in search of their own white island.* . . . He felt the warmth beneath him. The lips within this earth were smiling, caked in old gore, drawn out into the loveliest smile, male and female together, living and waiting.

His feet touched the base of the heap. One foot scraped the stiff snow from its side, clearing a space for him to stand. But he did not presume to take his position while clothed. 'I know you,' he whispered to the ground, 'I know you, I know you. . . .'

Setting down the story – still wrapped up in his jacket – he wrenched off his tie and tossed it on to the heap. His shirt followed. Without it he felt warmer. Then came his soiled shoes and socks. He reached into his trouser pocket for the packet of blades.

Now he would dance. Now the light would take his roar and show him the steps. The light painted him with its warmth, burning brightest against his waiting penis. He craved to be received. Supplicant, he stepped on to the space he had cleared for himself on the heap. Standing on the cool soil, his right foot planted higher than his left, he opened the paper packet in his hand. He picked out two blades. And after refolding the paper he tossed the packet on to his pile of clothes.

He held up the two blades in his right hand, as if to assure her eyes and her lips that this time he would not fail. Then he held up his left hand, flat and steady with its fingers pressed together. He slid the first blade between two of the fingers until it was wedged tightly. Holding the second blade in the thumb and third finger of that hand, he inserted it between two fingers on his right hand. He had no fear. He would use these blades. He was warm and he would use them, gladly, as a son of the sky.

Slowly, majestically, he stretched his arms to right and left, presenting himself to the fortress, to the smiling keeper of the gateway. The blades were safe between his fingers. They would not fall. He would not allow them to fall. With each arm at its full extent, he stared unblinking.

A cloud of light was bursting behind him. He was ready. The silent roar was coming from the surface of him. And he saw the shape of a woman.

'David,' she called, close amid the chaos of colour.

Her hand was reaching for his, and Nennius saw lips, parted so wide that the entire island of Albion was there between them.

'David,' she said again, her voice far richer now – the voice of a man.

And it was enough.

7

'David,' Rachel called a third time from just inside shed number twenty-one. There were perhaps ten yards between her and the compost-heap on which Nennius stood. She raised her other hand and said his name a fourth time, a fifth time, unable to keep the terror out of her voice.

She knew he couldn't see her. Where his eyes should have been there was only whiteness. But it seemed that he could hear. Still entranced, his arms stretched like wings, the razor blades lodged between the fingers of both hands, he stepped down slowly from the side of the heap.

Rachel swallowed. Birds wheeled and cawed above the skeletal trees which lined the horizon. As the rain eased the mist was seeping back, and Rachel looked in awe at Nennius' uncovered skin. *The uplands of Hell*, she remembered. And she dared to look beyond him at the heap under which she knew there lay a corpse. These, surely, were the uplands of Hell.

Nennius approached, undistressed, across the stony mud and bracken and old snow. 'I know you,' he murmured with a shy smile. 'I know you. . . .'

And as he came before her he allowed his arms to float back down to his sides. Rachel stepped back. Then he was inside the shed with her. And, in the transition between the dimness outside and the deeper darkness within, his eyes reappeared in his head, and he was looking directly at her. Rachel had entered his story.

She took another step back. It took her up on to the layers of rough-textured matting which she had found strewn on the hardboard floor. The rest of the shed's contents – gardening tools, flower-pots, seed-boxes – had been stacked neatly against the wooden walls. Rachel had remembered none of this tidiness from the night before. When she had come upon Nennius then, he had seemed hemmed in by all the paraphernalia.

The last of the rain pattered against the corrugated-iron roof. At any moment, Rachel knew, Nennius would see her for who she really was. He still had the razor blades. He was four, maybe five, feet away from her. This is a story, she tried to convince herself. I'm as unreal now as he is.

'David,' she cried again, losing her nerve and lurching forward. In a single step she was against him.

She threw her arms around his waist. Almost at once she felt his penis respond. His flesh was icy. Even through her duffel coat and top his coldness shocked her. He did not return her embrace. She drew herself back and, looking down, grasped both his wrists.

'I know you,' he whispered high, high, above her. 'I know you, I have found you. . . .'

'No!' Rachel cried, keeping hold of his wrists but pressing her face into his torso and kissing his marble skin. 'No, David, no!' Then she reached up, locked her fingers behind his neck and drew him down so that their mouths could meet.

He wanted the kisses that she gave him.

Soon he stopped simply taking, and he kissed her keenly in return. But his hands stayed by his sides, bristling with danger. Rachel stepped back, bringing him with her, until she was again on the bed of matting. Then she sank to her knees, kissing him as she sank, and again she took his wrists.

Both his hands were flat, rigid. 'Oh, Christ, David,' Rachel moaned. 'Please let go. Please, please, please let go. . . .'

But he sank down, too, and when their faces were almost level he searched out her mouth again. When he had finished with her mouth he kissed her tear-streaked cheeks and her eyes and her forehead, and then he said: 'I know you, I have found you, and I will not let you go.'

Rachel kissed his shoulder, hard. Her teeth scraped against his flesh. She clawed at his back, longing with the whole of herself for him not to die. It couldn't end like this. The despair and the pain and the beauty of his story, *their* story, couldn't be allowed to end in his blood.

'You've found *me*, David,' she wept. 'Rachel. Here. Just me. None of the rest of it.'

He raised his arms, and she felt the pressure of his elbows against her shoulders. She closed her eyes. Then she took the risk and twisted him down to her left.

He went with her, surprisingly easily, his hands still aloft, and she took most of his weight until his back was on the matting.

Quickly she was astride him, forcing out his arms until each awful hand was safely distant from its opposite wrist. His right arm was bent, the forearm pressing hard against one of the damp walls. Rachel, vertiginous now, beat his wrist against the wood until she heard the blade fall harmlessly against one of the flower-pots on the floor.

But with the hand which she had freed Nennius suddenly reached up, cupped her neck and drew her lips down on to his. There was force in this kissing. It made Rachel blench. She didn't want his passion in this way. It wasn't – she believed – the kind of love he needed. It wasn't the saving kind of love that she wished to offer.

'David,' she sobbed, rising from him and pushing herself back, then quivering as the shaft of his penis brushed the inside of her bare thigh. He reached for her again with his free hand, fingering her face and her heaving throat.

'Rachel,' he said with sudden clarity, and quite without accusation or dismay.

'Yes, David! Rachel,' she gasped through more tears. '*Yes! Yes.*'

In the weakness and relief of that moment, she stopped working against him and tore herself out of the story.

She was reaching beneath her coat and skirt, making herself open to him, weeping harder, knowing that one of his hands was still deadly. 'It's me,' she breathed, laughing, as he pushed himself up into her. 'Me: Rachel. I'm with you, I'm with you.'

He was thrusting hard, his hands far apart. He was not smiling but looking up with cool wonder into her eyes.

209

'Rachel,' he said twice more, splitting the name into two distinct syllables.

She leaned forward, took his face between her hands and kissed him until he was wet with her kisses.

He moved faster beneath her.

'There's no woman,' Rachel whispered into his cheek, moving for his pleasure. 'There's nothing but you, no one here but us.'

'Rachel,' he said. Then he spent himself, protractedly, and Rachel was smiling into his open eyes.

'Only you now,' she said, nodding. 'All the rest is lies.'

She laid her face against his, and watched the fingers of his left hand come apart, allowing the second razor blade to topple the short way to the safety of the floor.

Eventually Rachel's legs began to stiffen.

She eased herself off Nennius' gently trembling body and propped herself up on one elbow beside him.

He turned his head towards her and kissed the space between her eyes. His hair was dark with the rain. He hoisted himself on to his side and placed a hand on Rachel's higher shoulder.

'You,' Rachel said pointedly, sniffing, unable to smile.

He looked away and started to shudder.

Rachel sat up, pulled off her coat and laid it over the top half of his body. On him it looked absurd, a piece of doll's clothing.

'I'll fetch your things,' Rachel whispered. But as she pushed herself up from the matting Nennius caught her wrist.

Compliant, she remained where she was, poised between crouching and standing. But she continued to look out at the heap of compost, at the clothing on its side, all shrouded in the thickening mist and gloom.

'I killed him, Rachel,' Nennius said softly. 'And I buried him. Out there.' He breathed in, relaxed his hold on Rachel's wrist, and nodded in the direction in which Rachel was staring through fresh tears. 'That's no lie.'

Rachel stood. His song had come sawing back into her head. *No one knows what it's like. . . . No one knows. . . . No one. . . .*

Now that she had helped him to reach his rightful end, and he could say what he needed to say, she didn't want to hear. She had no wish to endorse what he had done, absolve him, bless him, ensure with words that this was – for him – a beginning as well as an end.

'I'll fetch your things,' she repeated. Moments before, she had come to an end of her own.

8

Shuddering less violently, Nennius watched Rachel leave the shed. In her thin top and skirt she hugged herself against the cold. Beyond her Nennius saw the gate and, propped against it, Melissa's old bicycle. Past that, all was grainy darkness.

Rachel stooped to pluck his garments from the heap. She looked solemn, reluctant – the first woman to whom he had made love since the loss of his wife; the only person, save Melissa, to whom he had ever dared speak of the killing. And he had said it. *Said* it. At the last, neither the love nor the words had been beyond him. They had come together: words and love, love and words. Now she was out there, his Good Samaritan, recovering his clothing.

But when Rachel lifted the folded jacket the sleeves flapped apart, and all the pages inside fanned down on to the churned ground. Nennius saw her lovely face crumple. Silently weeping, she tucked his damp clothes under one arm, kneeled, and started to reassemble his story.

'No,' Nennius called, leaning forward so that Rachel's duffel coat slid down into his lap.

She looked up. Their eyes met.

'Please,' Nennius said. 'Leave it.'

Rachel looked away. They both stood: Nennius in the shed, Rachel weeping outside it. Nennius held her coat in front of himself, and she came with his clothes. He extended one arm, encircled the girl's shoulder and drew her against him. She had allowed him to love her. It was she who had given him a way to say the words. Now she cried loudly, fighting to catch her breath. She cried for longer than it had taken them to make love

Nennius kissed the crown of her head. Still she bore a trace of perfume, a scent from a different day. Nennius could remember that kind of faintness. He had a purchase on himself. She had given him a purchase on himself. He kissed her head again, and, looking down past her, he saw a single razor blade on the ground by his bare foot. It made only the slightest sense now, where once it had seemed so perfect.

At length Rachel's sobbing quietened. Nennius draped the coat around her shoulders. She tried in vain to laugh, then wiped her face on a sleeve of his jacket. He took the bundle of clothes from her. 'My Good Samaritan,' he said slowly, watching her face.

At once Rachel turned away. 'Not any more.'

Nennius held out a hand to her again. But, whether she saw his gesture or not, she leaned against the shed's doorway, just out of his reach, and stared into the coming night.

Nennius dressed himself with the speed of shame. His shoes and the bottoms of his trousers were heavy with mud. But his shirt was drier than he had expected, his jacket damp only in places. He rolled up his tie and stuffed it into his pocket. From the other pocket he took a packet of cigarettes and a lighter.

Looking about him, he saw that the shed's interior had been rearranged since the night before. He saw it and, to his own sad satisfaction, he explained it. Then he prayed, hard: Forgive me for involving him.

He set two cigarettes between his lips, lit them, and stepped up behind Rachel. He held one cigarette just in front of her. She had folded her arms beneath the drape of her coat, and she shook her head, but Nennius wouldn't withdraw the cigarette. Rachel watched its thin trail of smoke, coiling through the whorls of her breath. She took the cigarette, delicately, between the tips of her finger and thumb.

'I never do,' she said without looking back at Nennius. 'Not ever.' And with a flick of her wrist she tossed it to the ground. They both watched it burn until its dim light died. Then Nennius stepped back.

He finished smoking his own cigarette, and ground its butt into the makeshift bed. *Quinn's* makeshift bed. For this, most surely, must have been Quinn's refuge during the previous night. There was nowhere else for him to have gone, nowhere more appropriate. At the end, like Nennius himself, poor Quinn had come back to the beginning. Forgive me, Nennius prayed again.

'I think', Rachel said suddenly, as if to the heap and the scatter of pages, 'we should go home.'

Nennius could only clear his throat. There was the suggestion of a glow out on the track. Rachel took the coat from her shoulders and slipped her arms into the sleeves. When Nennius came up behind her, she allowed herself to fall back against him. He placed his hands at her waist.

'Home,' she said again, huskily. 'You to yours. Me to mine.'

Nennius took his hands from her. He understood. It wasn't to be that kind of a beginning. Of course he would lose her. Everyone went. Everyone – from his father and mother to his wife and child, through to Quinn and now even Rachel. All of them. Only the dead stayed with him.

Nennius looked up, distracted by the hum of an approaching car. He saw the glow of its headlamps gathering strength through the mist, illuminating Melissa's bicycle. Rachel arched her back away from him. She left the shed, bent down and began to scoop up the pages. At once Nennius was beside her. Frowning, he took from her hands what she had already gathered.

'Why are you doing this?' he asked, sweeping up the other pages in random order, crumpling some, tearing others that had already been soaked through.

'There's no reason for Art to know,' she answered.

'Art?' Nennius squinted at her. 'Here?'

Rachel shrugged. She looked surfeited with him, used up with him and with everything to do with him. 'I left a message at the house.'

The car was easing to a halt near the gate, although it still couldn't be seen from Nennius' allotment.

Rachel looked at his fully laden hands. 'You'll see Art?'

Nennius glanced towards the gate, then back inside the shed. A high-speed train approached, shot past with a scream, and left them standing in a heightened silence.

You'll see Art? Her question stood unanswered between

them, pointing to the safer end, if not the simpler. Again Nennius glanced back into the shed. As a result of Quinn's reorganisation the garden tools were leaning against its far wall. He felt ashamed, reduced, but this girl's dispassionate love had at least begun to winnow away his guilt.

'Please,' he said, smiling, and dumping his pages into Rachel's arms.

He returned to the shed. On pulling aside the hoes and forks to reach the sturdiest spade, he found Quinn's rucksack. On top of it lay his crash-helmet. Nennius closed his eyes and prayed to God for a third time. Keep him safe, he pleaded. And bring him back.

Then, because it was all he could do, he took the spade outside and thrust it into that part of the heap from which he had previously cleared the snow. The surface was frozen stiff, but he dug out half a dozen great spadefuls. Silently he took the pages from Rachel, dropped them into the strange sarcophagus, and began to shovel back the disturbed compost.

Rachel looked away from Nennius to the gate. Beyond it two men stood in conversation – both tall, one far more slender than the other.

She looked back at Nennius, and longed for the word 'love' to pass between them, if only, after what they had just done, the word could have been wrenched free of its carnal connotations. For she had loved this man. Watching him beat down the compost with his spade, as the ruinous side of him yielded to a commonplace side that she had scarcely known, she loved him still.

But the stronger love, the love which had led her to this pass, had been an answer to his majestic despair. She had offered him her love, all her love in the end, because he had needed all of it to survive. And now, as she had realised back in the shed, she had to express the simplicity of this truth to a man who was, in his own way, just as desperate.

'I'm going, David,' she said, stepping away, noticing that one of the men was already climbing the gate.

Nennius threw the spade into the shed. He faced her. She didn't want to kiss him again. They didn't need to touch again. He seemed to have been growing younger all day, but the zeal had gone from his eyes. This wasn't the man who had raised his arms like wings, with razor blades for feathers. And, to Rachel's own disbelief, a tiny part of her regretted that.

She smiled, almost laughed. Don't say anything, she prayed at him. Don't go back to the words. She finished smiling, turned away, and broke into a trot as the more slender man splashed down into the mud inside the gate.

'Art?' she said.

He nodded, rubbing his hands together in the cold. He wore tight jeans and a short denim jacket. His face was round and freckled. And he looked, understandably in the circumstances, quite horribly diffident.

'I'm Rachel,' she said, acknowledging the bemused smile of the older man who stood on the far side of the gate. Then she looked back at Art, and pointed to the huge man who was still just visible. 'Your father's over there,' she said. 'He's waiting for you.'

The boy didn't move. He looked back over the gate at Meredith.

'Go on,' said the older man, nodding. 'Go on.'

As the boy set off across the snow, Rachel stepped closer to the gate. Meredith raised his eyebrows. He looked younger than Rachel had been expecting. 'What the hell are we doing here?' he laughed.

She didn't answer. Instead she looked over her shoulder to see Art coming before his father, offering his hand. When Nennius took Art's hand in both his own, she looked away.

'Would you help me over?' she said, stepping up on to the gate.

Meredith lifted her down on the other side. As soon as her feet touched the ground she clung to him, suddenly afraid that she was going to collapse.

'Hey now!' Meredith laughed. 'What's this?'

Rachel was crying again. She felt sure that she was going to be sick. But she just kept on crying into the lapel of Meredith's coat until he held her away from him, bent his knees and peered into her face.

'I'm sorry,' she hiccuped. 'I really am.' Then she put his hands away from her, and looked, again, over her shoulder

216

Nennius and Art still stood next to the heap. But where two distinct figures had previously been marked out against the snow there now seemed to be one larger blur. A flame flared. Rachel saw two faces, inches apart. Father and son lit their cigarettes. 'Please,' she said to Meredith. 'Could you take me home?'

'Sure.'

'Now?'

'Sure.' He sounded uncertain, and glanced at the allotment. Then he laid a hand on the saddle of Melissa's bicycle. 'Shall I put this in the boot?'

'It's not mine,' she told him, fumbling in her coat pocket for a tissue and finding only the packet of razor blades which she had picked up in the shed on the night before. She wiped her eyes and nose on her sleeve.

Meredith walked around to the driver's side of his car. He opened the door, but paused and then indicated Nennius' allotment. 'What about that pair?'

Rachel stepped up to the passenger-door. 'I should think they'll be able to find their own way.'

Meredith grinned. 'Where you want to go?'

Nennius and his son watched the car disappear down the track. They finished their cigarettes in silence. Then Nennius nodded, and they set off through the mud. As Art swung himself up on to the gate, Nennius glanced back at his allotment. Just to the side of the compost-heap, he saw movement.

It was a man, darting forward, merging with the large silhouette of the shed. Nennius narrowed his eyes and touched Art's leg. 'Wait,' he said.

The boy climbed down from the gate, still on the allotment side, and watched his father tramp back the way that they had just come.

Nennius stopped beside the heap. Directly in front of the shed door he could distinguish the outline of a man. He put out a hand, and walked on more tentatively. The man's face became clear. It was Quinn.

Nennius heard Art coming up behind him. He turned.

'It's all right,' he said to the frowning boy. There were only five or six yards between them. Nennius tried to smile. 'It's all right,' he repeated. 'Stay there.'

He turned back to Quinn, and again stepped forward, offering his hand. Quinn was close enough to have grasped it. But instead he looked away. Nennius shook his head, knowing that Art would hear everything they said. 'You don't,' he began, in little more than a whisper, 'you don't have to sleep here. . . .'

Quinn glanced in the direction of the railway line. He seemed, in profile, to be smiling.

'Come back to the house,' Nennius said. 'You must.'

Quinn's hands were in his jacket pockets, his chin pressed hard into his collarbone. Slowly he turned his head, until he was looking straight past Nennius.

Art called out. Just one anxious word: 'Dad?'

'It's all right,' Nennius called back, but this time his tone was less even. Helplessly the big man shook his head at Quinn. 'It's your house, too,' he said.

Quinn shifted his weight from foot to foot. He nodded, then looked up at last into Nennius' eyes. 'I'm here to collect my things, David,' he said quietly. 'I'm going.'

'The house, though . . . ,' Nennius insisted. 'Your room. . . .'

Quinn closed his eyes and smiled.

Nennius pinched the skin at the bridge of his nose. 'I don't want you to go,' he murmured.

Quinn's eyes were still closed. He appeared to shudder.

'I don't want you to go,' Nennius said again, more loudly.

Quinn's eyes were glinting now, not at Nennius but at the perplexed boy standing just behind him. He turned away and made to open the shed door.

At once Nennius moved closer. Quinn twisted round. Nennius laid his hand on Quinn's shoulder. The younger man swayed, stiffened, then stepped beyond his reach. As he did so he reached into his trouser pocket. He pulled out a doorkey and offered it up to Nennius, stiff-armed, defiant, as if he were exorcising him with a crucifix.

He nodded when Nennius took the key.

He nodded again, more vigorously, as Nennius continued

to gaze down at him.

'Oh, *go*,' Quinn breathed.

And then at last the big man nodded back, turned, and went to his son.

9

Meredith drove fast but safely across town. When Rachel finished drying her face and blowing her nose, he smiled at her. 'I don't suppose you'd fancy telling me what's been going on?' he said.

Rachel gazed out at the passing shops. She knew how dire she looked. She presumed that she stank of the shed, of dampness and dirt, of sex and stale perfume. 'I can't,' she said, dipping her head. 'Really. I can't.'

She saw him grin in resignation. But she had lied – it would have been easy to have explained it all to this stranger. Much easier than explaining it to Matthew. She liked Meredith's manner; she guessed that she could have trusted him with the truth. But he was the wrong man. She had to save her talk, and all her energy, for the man who was right.

Meredith turned on the radio. Rachel closed her eyes. It was over, yet she still knew so little of David Nennius, of the man at her side, of the precise connection between them. *Family*, Melissa had said, *of a sort. . . .*

They entered Matthew's road. Rachel guided Meredith towards a suitable place to stop – not outside the flat, in case Matthew was at the study window. As they drew up, she grasped a toggle on her coat and turned in her seat.

'William,' she said in a small voice. 'Are you and David related?'

'Not really,' he replied with a shrug. 'My parents took David in, that's all, after his mother died. . . . You look surprised. He hasn't told you about that?'

Rachel looked into his eyes until her look became a stare.

Meredith smiled. 'Well, there's no reason why he should have mentioned it,' he said. 'Is there?'

'Your father,' Rachel asked slowly, 'was your father called Emrys?'

'He was, love. David told you about him, then?'

'And you all lived in David's house? I mean, *your* house?'

He eyed her before answering. 'For a short time, yes. We all moved down when I was in my teens.' He eyed her again and shrugged. 'I soon went back north and got myself settled up there. Dad left me the house when he died, but by that time David had more use for it than I did.'

Rachel nodded. Melissa, with her own family out of the country, might well have retreated with her son to the man who was effectively her brother-in-law. It made a kind of sense. Then Meredith switched off the radio.

'Can *I* just get one · thing clear now, Rachel?' he said. 'It's about what you said on the phone last night, about why Melissa left David.' Rachel turned to him. He flicked a finger at the steering-wheel. Rachel waited. 'I mean, it's not the sort of thing you can go around saying.' He tried to grin. 'Is it?'

Rachel knew what she knew. There was no doubt in her mind about what Nennius had done. But she had no idea how to reply to Meredith's question. She started to wonder, as she searched his puzzled face, if perhaps he didn't know the full story himself.

It *was* remotely possible that Melissa had never told him the entire unspeakable truth. He had, after all, been so relaxed about letting Art go to his father at that place of burial. Yet Rachel no longer wanted to play with the possibilities. She just wanted to leave all of this behind.

'You're right,' she agreed, and she knew exactly what she meant when she added: 'It isn't the sort of thing you can go around saying.' She opened her door and pushed herself out on to the pavement. 'Thanks for the lift.'

Meredith smiled up at her. 'Perhaps we'll all meet up again some time now?'

Rachel smiled back, slammed the passenger-door and watched him drive away.

The flat was fifty yards further on up the road. Rachel

slowed her step as she approached the small glass-sided bus shelter. She didn't look at the packet of razor blades before dropping it into the litter-bin.

She kept her head down until she was inside the flat. All was quiet. There were no lights on save in the study, the door to which was ajar.

Standing in front of the hall mirror, she undid her coat. The front of her skirt was streaked with mud. She found more marks on her top, and even a smudge at her temple. But she didn't try to remove or conceal any of them. This filth would be a part of her presentation to Matthew. All along, the lies, the half-truths and the sad little suppressions had just been stretching the distance between them.

She crossed to the study doorway and smiled at Matthew's hunched back. She wanted to go through it all with him: beginning, middle and end. She was determined to stop cheapening their love by saying only what she knew her husband wanted to hear.

Matthew didn't turn. There were some papers in front of him, and a higher heap of pages to his right. For a crazy moment Rachel thought he was reading David Nennius' story. The phone, wrapped in its disconnected mains lead, lay on the small sofa-bed. Matthew drew back his head, lifted a page and placed it face down upon the heap.

Rachel walked to the sofa-bed, nudged the phone aside, sat down, and stared at the side of her husband's face. He hadn't shaved, but still he looked beautifully clean in his blue check shirt and cord jeans. She wanted to touch him. All she wanted to do – to begin with – was to stand against him, cling to him and smell the cleanness of him.

'Did Alasdair give you my message?' she asked.

Matthew flipped over another page. I love you, Rachel thought, I do, do love you. 'Matthew,' she said, locking her fingers over her knees. 'Did Alasdair come back here last night?'

Matthew picked up the heap of pages to his right, turned it over and dropped it down on to the page he had been reading. Rachel supposed that he had completed his secret story. She watched the movements of his smooth, long-fingered, guiltless hands as he aligned the pages' edges. She wanted to feel those hands on her face, her eyes, her clothes, her skin.

He pushed the story sideways, towards her. As she glanced at it, Matthew looked at her for the first time. His distress at her appearance was so clear that there was no need for him to say a word.

'Did Ally come here, Matthew?' Rachel asked once more.

Matthew nodded. 'What's happening, then, Rachel?' he asked her levelly. 'Are you leaving me?'

'I'm not leaving you,' Rachel told him, holding his gaze.

Matthew chuckled. 'Well, then,' he said, turning away in his chair. 'Well, then.' He placed the tips of his fingers on the story, then ran his thumb up and down its side, flicking at the pages.

Did he, Rachel asked herself, want her to say something about the fact that he had finished his thinly veiled autobiography? Or was he simply trying to tell her: Here's how I've been putting myself back together. Whatever you've been doing, I've been here, doing this, on my own. . . .

Matthew stood. He walked as far away from Rachel as he could, turned, and faced her. 'You've got yourself another man, then?' he said.

Rachel felt her face opening out. She looked from Matthew to the story and back at Matthew. 'I've got no one else,' she replied with a calmness which seemed to communicate itself, if only for a moment, to him. 'I've been with a client. The one who that young guy came to see me about.'

He raised his eyebrows at her. His face had reddened, but he said nothing. Rachel couldn't gauge his mood at all. *Silent as despairing love*, sidled back into her head, *and strong as.* . . . She raised a hand to her smeared temple to make the words go back. 'I want to talk to you about it,' she said.

'Oh,' he laughed. 'What can there be to talk about?'

'Sorry?' She looked at him, perplexed.

Matthew laughed again and shook his head, as if he were genuinely amused. 'Go on, then,' he said. 'Tell me all about it. Tell me it was both more and less than simply making love.'

Rachel closed her eyes. 'I want to explain to you. I want

to tell you what happened, and why it happened. I want us to *talk*, Matthew.'

He took a step towards her. For a moment he seemed to be all over the room. 'Just start at the end,' he said. 'You made love – yes?'

Suddenly, to her own astonishment, Rachel began to cry.

She cried with all of herself, but she had nothing to hold on to, so she came unsteadily to where Matthew was standing in his dismal unwanted triumph.

He brushed down her raised arms. Startled by his failure to respond to her tears, she looked up into his eyes.

'It's all I need to know, Rachel,' he said. 'You can start right in at the end. I don't want to know about the beginning or the middle.'

Rachel kept crying. She put the backs of both hands to her eyes.

'You chop away at everything,' she sobbed at Matthew in a strange hoarse voice. 'You cut everything down until it will fit into this flat. But you can't keep doing that. Oh, darling, we're a part of something bigger.' She blinked, then reached for his hands. 'There's got to be more *love* if any of us are going to go on.'

Matthew caught her by both wrists. 'Tell me,' he said, almost kindly, oblivious to everything but the need to have his question answered.

Rachel looked away, at his desk, at his story. There could be no more evasions and dilutions. She remembered those few minutes when David Nennius had been inside her. She remembered the discomfort and the stomach-clenching cold and the anxiety mixed with utter impersonal exultation of those few minutes. And she knew that she didn't have the vocabulary to put all that across, not here, not now, not to *this* Matthew.

'Yes,' she told her husband, seeing with his eyes everything that she had done. 'It did happen. We did make love, yes.'

Matthew let go of her left wrist. Then he struck her powerfully across the side of her face.

Rachel hadn't seen the blow coming. She tilted back in silence, but Matthew kept hold of her right wrist. He pulled her into an upright position, then he hit her again – this time, Rachel guessed from the blow's different quality, with his fist rather than with the flat of his hand. She made no sound. Davis sprang lamely from his basket and barked in panic beside them.

Matthew let go of her. She slumped back on to the sofa, her hands in her lap, her eyes closed tight. He had never used force on her before. She had never before told him that she had been with another man. It can't end here, she was shouting inside herself.

She heard Matthew and Davis leaving the room. Then she heard Matthew unlocking the back door and, with a stream of oaths, urging the dog out into the garden. Rachel opened her eyes and she thought of David Nennius, alive somewhere, taking a cigarette from his lips and nodding his head. And beyond the ticking of the wall clock she heard her husband crying. A harsh irregular sound. It couldn't end there.

She stood. Her legs were quite steady. Quietly she went to the doorway of their bedroom. Matthew – the real Matthew – lay curled on the bed facing her. 'Oh Christ,' he said, shuddering. 'Oh Christ, Rachel, oh Christ.'

She sat beside him and put her hand on his shoulder. She had to give him this chance to listen, and then the chance to talk back. She kissed his hair. She fell against him. She took him to herself at last.

And then she told him, in the best way that she knew, about the beginning and the middle of it all.

FOR THE BEST IN PAPERBACKS, LOOK FOR THE 🐧

In every corner of the world, on every subject under the sun, Penguin represents quality and variety – the very best in publishing today.

For complete information about books available from Penguin – including Puffins, Penguin Classics and Arkana – and how to order them, write to us at the appropriate address below. Please note that for copyright reasons the selection of books varies from country to country.

In the United Kingdom: Please write to *Dept E.P., Penguin Books Ltd, Harmondsworth, Middlesex, UB7 0DA.*

If you have any difficulty in obtaining a title, please send your order with the correct money, plus ten per cent for postage and packaging, to *PO Box No 11, West Drayton, Middlesex*

In the United States: Please write to *Dept BA, Penguin, 299 Murray Hill Parkway, East Rutherford, New Jersey 07073*

In Canada: Please write to *Penguin Books Canada Ltd, 2801 John Street, Markham, Ontario L3R 1B4*

In Australia: Please write to the *Marketing Department, Penguin Books Australia Ltd, P.O. Box 257, Ringwood, Victoria 3134*

In New Zealand: Please write to the *Marketing Department, Penguin Books (NZ) Ltd, Private Bag, Takapuna, Auckland 9*

In India: Please write to *Penguin Overseas Ltd, 706 Eros Apartments, 56 Nehru Place, New Delhi, 110019*

In the Netherlands: Please write to *Penguin Books Netherlands B.V., Postbus 195, NL–1380AD Weesp*

In West Germany: Please write to *Penguin Books Ltd, Friedrichstrasse 10–12, D–6000 Frankfurt/Main 1*

In Spain: Please write to *Longman Penguin España, Calle San Nicolas 15, E–28013 Madrid*

In Italy: Please write to *Penguin Italia s.r.l., Via Como 4, I-20096 Pioltello (Milano)*

In France: Please write to *Penguin Books Ltd, 39 Rue de Montmorency, F-75003 Paris*

In Japan: Please write to *Longman Penguin Japan Co Ltd, Yamaguchi Building, 2–12–9 Kanda Jimbocho, Chiyoda-Ku, Tokyo 101*